SUICIDE RACE TO LUNA

The four men had been scrutinized, watched, investigated, and intensively trained for more than a year. They were the best men to be found for that first, all-important flight to the Moon—the pioneer manned rocket that would give either the East or the West control over the Earth.

Yet when the race started, Adam Crag found that he had a saboteur among his crew . . . a traitor! Such a man could give the Reds possession of Luna, and thereby dominate the world it circled.

Any one of the other three could be the hidden enemy, and if he didn't discover the agent soon—even while they were roaring on rocket jets through outer space—then Adam Crag, his expedition, and his country would be destroyed!

JEFF SUTTON, although experienced in journalistic and technical writings, has only recently turned his hand to novels with the result that *First on the Moon* is also his first novel. A native Californian, and a Marine veteran, he is presently employed as a research engineer for Convair-San Diego, specializing appropriately enough for this novel in problems of high altitude survival. He says of himself:

"I have long been a science-fiction reader (a common ailment among scientists and engineers). On the personal side, a number of factors have coalesced to pin me to the typewriter. I am living in—and working in—a world of missiles, rockets, and far-reaching dreams. In many areas the border between science-fiction and science suddenly has become a lace curtain. It is a world I have some acquaintance with—and fits very nicely into my desire to write."

FIRST on the MOON

by
JEFF SUTTON

ACE BOOKS, INC.
23 West 47th Street, New York 36, N. Y.

FIRST ON THE MOON

Copyright ©, 1958, by Ace Books, Inc.

All Rights Reserved

To Sandy

Printed in U. S. A.

PROLOGUE

ONE OF THE rockets was silver; three were ashen gray. Each nested in a different spot on the great Western Desert. All were long, tapered, sisters except for color. In a way they represented the first, and last, of an era, with exotic propellants, a high mass ratio and three-stage design. Yet they were not quite alike. One of the sisters had within her the artifacts the human kind needed for life—a space cabin high in the nose. The remaining sisters were drones, beasts of burden, but beasts which carried scant payloads considering their bulk.

One thing they had in common—destination. They rested on their launch pads, with scaffolds almost cleared, heads high and proud. Soon they would flash skyward, one by one, seeking a relatively small haven on a strange bleak world. The world was the moon; the bleak place was called Arzachel, a crater—stark, alien, with tall cliffs brooding over an ashy plain.

Out on the West Coast a successor to the sisters was shaping up—a great ship of a new age, with nuclear drive and a single stage. But the sisters could not wait for their successor. Time was running out. . . .

CHAPTER I

THE ROOM was like a prison—at least to Adam Crag. It was a square with a narrow bunk, a battered desk, two straight-back chairs and little else. Its one small window overlooked the myriad quonsets and buildings of Burning Sands Base from the second floor of a nearly empty dormitory.

There was a sentry at the front of the building, another at the rear. Silent alert men who never spoke to Crag—seldom acknowledged his movements to and from the building—yet never let a stranger approach the weathered dorm without sharp challenge. Night and day they were there. From his window he could see the distant launch site and, by night, the batteries of floodlights illumining the metal monster on the pad. But now he wasn't thinking of the rocket. He was fretting; fuming because of a call from Colonel Michael Gotch.

"Don't stir from the room," Gotch had crisply ordered on the phone. He had hung up without explanation. That had been two hours before.

Crag had finished dressing—he had a date—idly wondering what was in the Colonel's mind. The fretting had only set in when, after more than an hour, Gotch had failed to show. Greg's liberty had been restricted to one night a month. One measly night, he thought. Now he was wasting it, tossing away the precious hours. Waiting. Waiting for what?

"I'm a slave," he told himself viciously; "slave to a damned bird colonel." His date wouldn't wait—wasn't the waiting kind. But he couldn't leave.

He stopped pacing long enough to look at himself in the cracked mirror above his desk. The face that stared back was lean, hard, unlined—skin that told of wind and sun, not brown nor bronze but more of a mahogany red. Just now the face was frowning. The eyes were wide-spaced, hazel, the nose arrogant and hawkish. A thin white scar ran over one cheek ending . . .

His mind registered movement behind him. He swiveled around, flexing his body, balanced on his toes . . . then relaxed, slightly mortified.

Gotch—Colonel Michael Gotch—stood just inside the door eyeing him tolerantly. A flush crept over Crag's face. Damn Gotch and his velvet feet, he thought. But he kept the thought concealed.

The expression on Gotch's face was replaced by a wooden mask. He studied the lean man by the mirror for a moment, then flipped his cap on the bed and sat down without switching his eyes.

He said succinctly. "You're it."

"I've got it?" Crag gave an audible sigh of relief. Gotch nodded without speaking.

"What about Temple?"

"Killed last night—flattened by a truck that came over the center-line. On an almost deserted highway just outside the base," Gotch added. He spoke casually but his eyes were not casual. They were unfathomable black pools. Opaque and hard. Crag wrinkled his brow inquiringly.

"Accident?"

"You know better than that. The truck was hot, a semi with bum plates, and no driver when the cops got there." His voice turned harsh. "No . . . it was no accident."

"I'm sorry," Crag said quietly. He hadn't known Temple personally. He had been just a name—a whispered name. One of three names, to be exact: Romer, Temple, Crag. Each had been hand-picked as possible pilots of the Aztec, a modified missile being rushed to completion in a last ditch effort to beat the Eastern World in the race for the moon. They had been separately indoctrinated, tested, trained; each had virtually lived in one of the scale-size simulators of the Aztec's space cabin, and had been rigorously schooled for the operation secretly referred to as "Step One." But they had been kept carefully apart. There had been a time when no one—unless it were the grim-faced Gotch—knew which of the three was first choice.

Romer had died first—killed as a bystander in a brawl. So the police said. Crag had suspected differently. Now Temple. The choice, after all, had not been the swarthy Colonel's to make. Somehow the knowledge pleased him. Gotch interrupted his thoughts.

"Things are happening. The chips are down. Time has run out, Adam." While he clipped the words out he weighed Crag, as if seeking some clue to his thoughts. His face said that everything now depended upon the lean man with the hairline scar across his cheek. His eyes momentarily wondered if the lean man could perform what man never before had done. But his lips didn't voice the doubt. After a moment he said:

"We know the East is behind us in developing an atomic spaceship. Quite a bit behind. We picked up a lot from some of our atomic sub work—that and our big missiles. But maybe the knowledge made us lax." He added stridently:

"Now . . . they're ready to launch."

"Now?"

"Now!"

"I didn't think they were that close."

"Intelligence tells us they've modified a couple of T-3's—the big ICBM model. We just got a line on it . . . almost too late." Gotch smiled bleakly. "So we've jumped our schedule, at great risk. It's your baby," he added.

Crag said simply: "I'm glad of the chance."

"You should be. You've hung around long enough," Gotch said dryly. His eyes probed Crag. "I only hope you've learned enough . . . are ready."

"Plenty ready," snapped Crag.

"I hope so."

Gotch got to his feet, a square fiftyish man with cropped iron-gray hair, thick shoulders and weather-roughened skin. Clearly he wasn't a desk colonel.

"You've got a job, Adam." His voice was unexpectedly soft but he continued to weigh Crag for a long moment before he picked up his cap and turned toward the door.

"Wait," he said. He paused, listening for a moment before he opened it, then slipped quietly into the hall, closing the door carefully behind him.

He's like a cat, Crag thought for the thousandth time, watching the closed door. He was a man who seemed forever listening; a heavy hulking man who walked on velvet feet; a man with opaque eyes who saw everything and told nothing. Gotch would return.

Despite the fact the grizzled Colonel had been his mentor for over a year he felt he hardly knew the man. He was high up in the missile program—missile security, Crag had supposed —yet he seemed to hold power far greater than that of a security officer. He seemed, in fact, to have full charge of the Aztec project—Step One—even though Dr. Kenneth Walmsbelt was its official director. The difference was, the nation knew Walmsbelt. He talked with congressmen, pleaded for money, carried his program to the newspapers and was a familiar figure on the country's TV screens. He was the leading exponent of the space-can't-wait philosophy. But few people knew Gotch; and fewer yet his connections. He was capable, competent, and to Crag's way of thinking, a tough monkey, which pretty well summarized his knowledge of the man.

He felt the elation welling inside him, growing until it was almost a painful pleasure. It had been born of months and months of hope, over a year during which he had scarcely dared hope. Now, because a man had died . . .

He sat looking at the ceiling, thinking, trying to still the inner tumult. Only outwardly was he calm. He heard footsteps returning. Gotch opened the door and entered, followed by a second man. Crag started involuntarily, half-rising from his chair.

He was looking at himself!

"Crag, meet Adam Crag." The Colonel's voice and face were expressionless. Crag extended his hand, feeling a little silly.

"Glad to know you."

The newcomer acknowledged the introduction with a grin —the same kind of lopsided grin the real Crag wore. More startling was the selfsame hairline scar traversing his cheek; the same touch of cockiness in the set of his face.

Gotch said, "I just wanted you to get a good look at yourself. Crag here"—he motioned his hand toward the newcomer—"is your official double. What were you planning for tonight, your last night on earth?"

"I have a date with Ann. Or had," he added sourly. He twisted his head toward Gotch as the Colonel's words sunk home. "Last night?"

Gotch disregarded the question. "For what?"

"Supper and dancing at the Blue Door."

"Then?"

"Take her home, if it's any of your damned business," snapped Crag. "I wasn't planning on staying, if that's what you mean."

"I know . . . I know, we have you on a chart," Gotch said amiably. "We know every move you've made since you wet your first diapers. Like that curvy little brunette secretary out in San Diego, or that blonde night club warbler you were rushing in Las Vegas." Crag flushed. The Colonel eyed him tolerantly.

"And plenty more," he added. He glanced at Crag's double. "I'm sure your twin will be happy to fill in for you tonight."

"Like hell he will," gritted Crag. The room was quiet for a moment.

"As I said, he'll fill in for you."

Crag grinned crookedly. "Ann won't go for it. She's used to the real article."

"We're not giving her a chance to snafu the works," Gotch said grimly. "She's in protective custody. We have a double for her, too."

"Mind explaining?"

"Not a bit. Let's face the facts and admit both Romer and Temple were murdered. That leaves only you. The enemy isn't about to let us get the Aztec into space. You're the only pilot left who's been trained for the big jump—the only man with the specialized know-how. That's why you're on someone's list. Perhaps, even, someone here at the Base . . . or on the highway . . . or in town. I don't know when or how but I do know this: You're a marked monkey."

Gotch added flatly: "I don't propose to let you get murdered."

"How about him?" Crag nodded toward his double. The man smiled faintly.

"That's what he's paid for," Gotch said unfeelingly. His lips curled sardonically. "All the heroes aren't in space."

Crag flushed. Gotch had a way of making him uncomfortable as no other man ever had. The gentle needle. But it was true. The Aztec was his baby. Gotch's role was to see that he lived long enough to get it into space. The rest was up to him. Something about the situation struck him as humorous. He looked at his double with a wry grin.

"Home and to bed early," he cautioned. "Don't forget you've got my reputation to uphold."

"Go to hell," his double said amiably.

"Okay, let's get down to business," Gotch growled. "I've got a little to say."

Long after they left Crag stood at the small window, looking out over the desert. Somewhere out there was the Aztec, a silver arrow crouched in its cradle, its nose pointed toward the stars. He drew the picture in his mind. She stood on her tail fins; a six-story-tall needle braced by metal catwalks and guard rails; a cousin twice-removed to the great nuclear weapons which guarded Fortress America. He had seen her at night, under the batteries of floor lights, agleam with a milky radiance; a virgin looking skyward, which, in fact, she was. Midway along her length her diameter tapered abruptly, tapered again beyond the three-quarters point. Her nose looked slender compared with her body, yet it contained a space cabin with all the panoply needed to sustain life beyond the atmosphere.

His thoughts were reverent, if not loving. Save for occasional too-brief intervals with Ann, the ship had dominated his life for over a year. He knew her more intimately, he thought, than a long-married man knows his wife.

He had never ceased to marvel at the Aztec's complexity. Everything about the rocket spoke of the future. She was clearly designed to perform in a time not yet come, at a place not yet known. She would fly, watching the stars, continuously measuring the angle between them, computing her way through the abyss of space. Like a woman she would understand the deep currents within her, the introspective sensing of every force which had an effect upon her life. She would measure gravitation, acceleration and angular velocity with infinite precision. She would count these as units of time, perform complex mathematical equations, translate them into course data, and find her way unerringly across the purple-black night which separated her from her assignation with destiny. She would move with the certainty of a woman fleeing to her lover. Yes, he thought, he would put his life in the lady's hands. He would ride with her on swift wings. But he would be her master.

His mood changed. He turned from the window thinking it was a hell of a way to spend his last night. Last night on earth, he corrected wryly. He couldn't leave the room, couldn't budge, didn't know where Ann was. No telephone. He went to bed wondering how he'd ever let himself get snookered into the deal. Here he was, young, with a zest for life and a stacked-up gal on the string. And what was he doing about it? Going to the moon, that's what. Going to some damned hell-hole called Arzachel, all because a smooth bird colonel had pitched him a few soft words. Sucker!

His lips twisted in a crooked grin. Gotch had seduced him by describing his mission as an "out-of-this-world opportunity." Those had been Gotch's words. Well, that was Arzachel. And pretty quick it would be Adam Crag. Out-of-this-world Crag. Just now the thought wasn't so appealing.

Sleep didn't come easy. At Gotch's orders he had turned in early, at the unheard hour of seven. Getting to sleep was another matter. It's strange, he thought, he didn't have any of the feelings Doc Weldon, the psychiatrist, had warned him of. He wasn't nervous, wasn't afraid. Yet before another sun had set he'd be driving the Aztec up from earth, into the loneliness of space, to a bleak crater named Arzachel. He would face the dangers of intense cosmic radiation, chance meteor swarms, and human errors in calculation which could spell disaster. It would be the first step in the world race for control of the Solar System—a crucial race with the small nations of the world watching for the winner. Watching and waiting to see which way to lean.

He was already cut off from mankind, imprisoned in a

small room with the momentous zero hour drawing steadily nearer. Strange, he thought, there had been a time when his career had seemed ended, washed up, finished, the magic of the stratosphere behind him for good. Sure, he'd resigned from the Air Force at his own free will, even if his C. O. had made the pointed suggestion. Because he hadn't blindly followed orders. Because he'd believed in making his own decisions when the chips were down. "Lack of *esprit de corps*," his C. O. had termed it.

He'd been surprised that night—it was over a year ago now—that Colonel Gotch had contacted him. (Just when he was wondering where he might get a job. He hadn't liked the prosaic prospects of pushing passengers around the country in some jet job.) Sure, he'd jumped at the offer. But the question had never left his mind. *Why had Gotch selected him?* The Aztec, a silver needle plunging through space followed by her drones, all in his tender care. He was planning the step-by-step procedure of take-off when sleep came.

CHAPTER 2

CRAG WOKE with a start, sensing he was not alone. The sound came again—a key being fitted into a lock. He started from bed as the door swung open.

"Easy. It's me—Gotch." Crag relaxed. A square solid figure took form.

"Don't turn on the light."

"Okay. What gives?"

"One moment." Gotch turned back toward the door and beckoned. Another figure glided into the room—a shadow in the dim light. Crag caught the glint of a uniform. Air Force officer, he thought.

Gotch said crisply; "Out of bed."

He climbed out, standing alongside the bed in his shorts, wondering at the Colonel's cloak-and-dagger approach.

"Okay, Major, it's your turn," Gotch said.

The newcomer—Crag saw he was a major—methodically stripped down to his shorts and got into bed without a word. Crag grinned, wondering how the Major liked his part in Step One. It was scarcely a lead role.

Gotch cut into his thoughts. "Get dressed." He indicated the Major's uniform. Crag donned the garments silently. When he had finished the Colonel walked around him in the dark, studying him from all angles.

"Seems to fit very well," he said finally. "All right, let's go."

Crag followed him from the room wondering what the unknown Major must be thinking. He wanted to ask about his double but refrained. Long ago he had learned there was a time to talk, and a time to keep quiet. This was the quiet time. At the outer door four soldiers sprang from the darkness and boxed them in. A chauffeur jumped from a waiting car and opened the rear door. At the last moment Crag stepped aside and made a mock bow.

"After you, Colonel." His voice held a touch of sarcasm.

Gotch grunted and climbed into the rear seat and he followed. The chauffeur blinked his lights twice before starting the engine. Somewhere ahead a car pulled away from the curb. They followed, leaving the four soldiers behind. Crag twisted his body and looked curiously out the rear window. Another car dogged their wake. Precautions, always precautions, he thought. Gotch had entered with an Air Force officer and had ostensibly left with one; ergo, it must be the same officer. He chuckled, thinking he had more doubles than a movie star.

They sped through the night with the escorts fore and aft. Gotch was a silent hulking form on the seat beside him. It's his zero hour, too, Crag thought. The Colonel had tossed the dice. Now he was waiting for their fall, with his career in the pot. After a while Gotch said conversationally:

"You'll report in at Albrook, Major. I imagine you'll be getting in a bit of flying from here on out."

Talking for the chauffeur's benefit, Crag thought. Good Lord, did every move have to be cloak and dagger? Aloud he said:

"Be good to get back in the air again. Perhaps anti-sub patrol, eh?"

"Very likely."

They fell silent again. The car skimmed west on Highway 80, leaving the silver rocket farther behind with every mile. Where to and what next? He gave up trying to figure the Colonel's strategy. One thing he was sure of. The hard-faced man next to him knew exactly what he was doing. If it was secret agent stuff, then that's the way it had to be played.

He leaned back and thought of the task ahead—the rocket he had lived with for over a year. Now the marriage would be consummated. Every detail of the Aztec was vivid in his mind. Like the three great motors tucked triangularly between her tail fins, each a tank equipped with a flaring nozzle to feed in hot gases under pressure. He pictured the fuel tanks just forward of the engines; the way the fuels were mixed, vaporized, forced into the fireports where they would ignite and react explosively, generating the enormous volumes of flaming hot gas to drive out through the jet tubes and provide the tremendous thrust needed to boost her into the skies. Between the engines and fuel tanks was a maze of machinery—fuel lines, speed controllers, electric motors.

He let his mind rove over the rocket thinking that before many hours had passed he would need every morsel of the knowledge he had so carefully gathered. Midway where the hull tapered was a joint, the separation point between the first and second stages. The second stage had one engine fed by two tanks. The exterior of the second stage was smooth, finless, for it was designed to operate at the fringe of space where the air molecules were widely spaced; but it could be steered by small deflectors mounted in its blast stream.

The third stage was little more than a space cabin riding between the tapered nose cone and a single relatively low-thrust engine. Between the engine and tanks was a maze of turbines, pumps, meters, motors, wires. A generator provided electricity for the ship's electric and electronic equipment; this in turn was spun by a turbine driven by the explosive decomposition of hydrogen peroxide. Forward of this was the Brain, a complex guidance mechanism which monitored engine performance, kept track of speed, computed course. All that was needed was the human hand. His hand.

They traveled several hours with only occasional words, purring across the flat sandy wastes at a steady seventy. The cars boxing them in kept at a steady distance.

Crag watched the yellow headlights sweep across the sage lining the highway, giving an odd illusion of movement. Light and shadow danced in eerie patterns. The chauffeur turned onto a two-lane road heading north. Alpine Base, Crag thought. He had been stationed there several years before. Now it was reputed to be the launch site of one of the three drones slated to cross the gulfs of space. The chauffeur drove past a housing area and turned in the direction he knew the strip to be.

Somewhere in the darkness ahead a drone brooded on its pad, one of the children of the silver missile they'd left behind. But why the drone? The question bothered him. They were stopped several times in the next half mile. Each time

Gotch gave his name and rank and extended his credentials. Each time they were waved on by silent sharp-eyed sentries, but only after an exacting scrutiny Crag was groping for answers when the chauffeur pulled to one side of the road and stopped. He leaped out and opened the rear door, standing silently to one side. When they emerged, he got back into the car and drove away. No word had been spoken. Figures moved toward them, coming out of the blackness.

"Stand where you are and be recognized." The figures took shape—soldiers with leveled rifles. They stood very still until one wearing a captain's bars approached, flashing a light in their faces.

"Identity?"

Crag's companion extended his credentials.

"Colonel Michael Gotch," he monotoned. The Captain turned the light on Gotch's face to compare it with the picture on the identification card. He paid scant attention to Crag. Finally he looked up.

"Proceed, Sir." It was evident the Colonel's guest was very much expected.

Gotch struck off through the darkness with Crag at his heels. The stars shone with icy brilliance. Overhead Antares stared down from its lair in Scorpio, blinking with fearful venom. The smell of sage filled the air, and some sweet elusive odor Crag couldn't identify. A warmth stole upward as the furnace of the desert gave up its stored heat. He strained his eyes into the darkness; stars, the black desert . . . and the hulking form of Gotch, moving with certain steps.

He saw the rocket with startling suddenness—a great black silhouette blotting out a segment of the stars. It stood gigantic, towering, graceful, a taper-nosed monster crouched to spring, its finned haunches squatted against the launch pad.

They were stopped, challenged, allowed to proceed. Crag pondered the reason for their visit to the drone. Gotch, he knew, had a good reason for every move he made. They drew nearer and he saw that most of the catwalks, guardrails and metal supports had been removed—a certain sign that the giant before them was near its zero hour.

Another sentry gave challenge at the base of the behemoth. Crag whistled to himself. This one wore the silver leaf of a lieutenant colonel! The ritual of identification was exacting before the sentry moved aside. A ladder zigzagged upward through what skeletal framework still remained. Crag lifted his eyes. It terminated high up, near the nose.

This was the Aztec! The real Aztec! The truth came in a rush. The huge silver ship at Burning Sands, which bore the name Aztec, was merely a fake, a subterfuge, a pawn in the complex game of agents and counter-agents. He knew he was right.

"After you," Gotch said. He indicated the ladder and stepped aside.

Crag started up. He paused at the third platform. The floor of the desert was a sea of darkness. Off in the distance the lights of Alpine Base gleamed, stark against the night. Gotch reached his level and laid a restraining hand on his arm.

Crag turned and waited. The Colonel's massive form was a black shadow interposed between him and the lights of Alpine Base.

"This is the Aztec," he said simply.

"So I guessed. And the silver job at Burning Sands?"

"Drone Able," Gotch explained. "The deception was necessary—a part of the cat and mouse game we've been playing the last couple of decades. We couldn't take a single chance." Crag remained silent. The Colonel turned toward the lights of the Base. He had become quiet, reflective. When he spoke, his voice was soft, almost like a man talking to himself.

"Out there are hundreds of men who have given a large

part of their lives to the dream of space flight. Now we are at the eve of making that dream live. If we gain the moon, we gain the planets. That's the destiny of Man. The Aztec is the first step." He turned back and faced Crag.

"This is but one base. There are many others. Beyond them are the factories, laboratories, colleges, scientists and engineers, right down to Joe the Riveter. Every one of them has had a part in the dream. You're another part, Adam, but you happen to have the lead role." He swiveled around and looked silently at the distant lights. The moment was solemn. A slight shiver ran through Crag's body.

"You know and I know that the Aztec is a development from the ICBM's guarding Fortress America. You also know, or have heard, that out in San Diego the first atom-powered spaceship is nearing completion." He looked sharply at Crag.

"I've heard," Crag said noncommittally.

Gotch eyed him steadily. "That's the point. So have others. Our space program is no secret. But we've suspected—feared—that the first stab at deep space would be made before the atom job was completed. Not satellites but deep space rockets. That's why the Aztec was pushed through so fast." He fell silent. Crag waited.

"Well, the worst has happened. The enemy is ready to launch—may have launched this very night. That's how close it is. Fortunately our gamble with the Aztec is paying off We're ready, too, Adam.

"We're going to get that moon. Get it now!" He reached into a pocket and extracted his pipe, then thought better of lighting it. Crag waited. The Colonel was in a rare introspective mood, a quiet moment in which he mentally tied together and weighed his Nation's prospects in the frightening days ahead. Finally he spoke:

"We put a rocket around the moon, Adam." He smiled faintly, noting Crag's involuntary start of surprise. "Naturally it was fully instrumented. There's uranium there—one big load located in the most inaccessible spot imaginable."

"Arzachel," Crag said simply.

"The south side of Arzachel, to be exact. That's why we didn't pick a soft touch like Mare Imbrium, in case you've wondered."

"I've wondered."

"Adam," the Colonel hesitated a long moment, "does the name Pickering mean anything to you?"

"Ken Pickering who—"

"What have you heard?" snapped Gotch. His eyes became sharp drills.

Crag spoke slowly: "Nothing . . . for a long time. He just seemed to drop oue of sight after he broke the altitude record in the X-34." He looked up questioningly.

"Frankly, I've always wondered why he hadn't been selected for this job. I thought he was a better pilot than I am," he added almost humbly.

Gotch said bluntly: "You're right. He is better." He smiled tolerantly. "We picked our men for particular jobs," he said finally. "Pickering . . . we hope . . . will be in orbit before the Aztec blasts off."

"Satelloid?"

"The first true satelloid," the Colonel agreed. "One that can ride the fringes of space around the earth. A satelloid with fantastic altitude and speed. I'm telling you this because he'll be a link in Step One, a communication and observation link. He won't be up long, of course, but long enough—we hope."

Silence fell between them. Crag looked past the Colonel's shoulder. All at once the lights of Alpine Base seemed warm and near, almost personal. Gotch lifted his eyes skyward, symbolic of his dreams. The light of distant stars reflected off his brow.

"We don't know whether the Aztec can make it," he said

humbly. "We don't know whether our space-lift system will work, whether the drones can be monitored down to such a precise point on the moon, or the dangers of meteorite bombardment. We don't know whether our safeguards for human life are adequate. We don't know whether the opposition can stop us. . . .

"We don't know lots of things, Adam. All we know is that we need the moon. It's a matter of survival of Western Man, his culture, his way of life, his political integrity. We need the moon to conquer the planets . . . and some day the stars."

His voice became a harsh clang.

"So does the enemy. That's why we have to establish a proprietory ownership, a claim that the U.N. will recognize. The little nations represent the balance of power, Adam. But they sway with the political winds. They are the reeds of power politics . . . swaying between the Sputniks and Explorers, riding with the ebb and flow of power . . . always trying to anticipate the ultimate winner. Right now they're watching to see where that power lies. The nation that wins the moon will tilt the balance in its favor. At a critical time, I might add. That's why we have to protect ourselves every inch of the way."

He tapped his cold pipe moodily against his hand. "We won't be here to see the end results, of course. That won't be in our time. But we're the starters. The Aztec is the pioneer ship. And in the future our economy can use that load of uranium up there."

He smiled faintly at Crag. "When you step through the hatch you've left earth, perhaps for all time. That's your part in the plan. Step One is your baby and I have confidence in you." He gripped Crag's arm warmly. It was the closest he had ever come to showing his feelings toward the man he was sending into space.

"Come on, let's go."

Crag started upward. Gotch followed more slowly, climbing like a man bearing a heavy weight.

The Aztec's crew, Max Prochaska, Gordon Nagel and Martin Larkwell, came aboard the rocket in the last hour before take-off. Gotch escorted them up the ladder and introduced them to their new Commander.

Prochaska acknowledged the introduction with a cheerful smile.

"Glad to know you, Skipper." His thin warm face said he was glad to be there.

Gordon Nagel gave a perfunctory handshake, taking in the space cabin with quick ferret-like head movements.

Martin Larkwell smiled genially, pumping Crag's hand. "I've been looking forward to this."

Crag said dryly. "We all have." He acknowledged the introductions with the distinct feeling that he already knew each member of his crew. It was the odd feeling of meeting old acquaintances after long years of separation. As part of his indoctrination he had studied the personnel records of the men he might be so dependent on. Now, seeing them in the flesh, was merely an act of giving life to those selfsame records. He studied them with casual eyes while Gotch rambled toward an awkward farewell.

Max Prochaska, his electronics chief, was a slender man with sparse brown hair, a thin acquiline nose and pointed jaw. His pale blue eyes, thin lips and alabaster skin gave him a delicate look—one belied by his record. His chief asset—if one was to believe the record—was that he was a genius in electronics.

Gordon Nagel, too, was thin-faced and pallid skinned. His black hair, normally long and wavy, had been close-cropped. His eyes were small, shifting, agate-black, giving Crag the feeling that he was uneasy—an impression he was to hold. His record had described him as nervous in manner but his psychograph was smooth. He was an expert in oxygen systems.

Martin Larkwell, the mechanical maintenance and construction boss, in many ways appeared the antithesis of his two companions. He was moon-faced, dark, with short brown hair and a deceptively sleepy look. His round body was well-muscled, his hands big and square. Crag thought of a sleek drowsy cat, until he saw his eyes. They were sparkling brown pools, glittering, moving with some strange inner fire. They were the eyes of a dreamer . . . or a fanatic, he thought. In the cabin's soft light they glowed, flickered. No, there was nothing sleepy about him, he decided.

All of the men were short, light, in their early thirties. In contrast Crag, at 5' 10" and 165 pounds, seemed a veritably giant. A small physique, he knew, was almost an essential in space, where every ounce was bought at tremendous added weight in fuel. His own weight had been a serious strike against him.

Colonel Gotch made one final trip to the space cabin. This time he brought the *Moon Code Manual* (stamped TOP SECRET), the crew personnel records (Crag wondered why) and a newly printed pamphlet titled "Moon Survival." Crag grinned when he saw it.

"Does it tell us how to get there, too?"

"We'll write that chapter later," Gotch grunted. He shook each man's hand and gruffly wished them luck before turning abruptly toward the hatch. He started down the ladder. A moment later his head reappeared.

He looked sharply at Crag and said, "By the way, that twosome at the Blue Door got it last night."

"You mean . . . ?"

"Burp gun. No finesse. Just sheer desperation. Well, I just wanted to let you know we weren't altogether crazy."

"I didn't think you were."

The Colonel's lips wrinkled in a curious smile. "No?" He

looked at Crag for a long moment. "Good luck." His head disappeared from view and Crag heard his footsteps descending the ladder.

Then they were alone, four men alone. Crag turned toward his companions.

CHAPTER 3

THE GREAT red sun was just breaking over the desert horizon when Crag got his last good look at earth. Its rays slanted upward, shadows fled from the sage; the obsidian sky with its strewn diamonds became slate gray and, in moments, a pale washed blue. Daybreak over the desert became a thunder of light. Tiny ants had removed the last of the metal framework encompassing the rocket. Other ants were visible making last minute checks.

He returned his attention to the space cabin. Despite long months of training in the cabin simulator—an exact replica of the Aztec quarters—he was appalled at the lack of outside vision. One narrow rectangular quartz window above the control panel, a circular port on each side bulkhead and one on the floor—he had to look between his knees to see through it when seated at the controls—provided the sole visual access to the outside world. A single large radarscope, a radar altimeter and other electronic equipment provided analogs of the outside world; the reconstruction of the exterior environment painted on the scopes by electromagnetic impulses.

The cabin was little more than a long flat-floored cylinder

with most of the instrumentation in the nose section. With the rocket in launch position, what normally was the rear wall formed the floor. The seats had been swiveled out to operational position.

Now they were seated, strapped down, waiting. It was, Crag thought, like sitting in a large automobile which had been balanced on its rear bumper. During launch and climb their backs would be horizontal to the earth's surface.

He was thankful they were not required to wear their heavy pressure suits until well into the moon's gravisphere. Normally pressure suits and helmets were the order of the day. He was used to stratospheric flight where heavy pressure suits and helmets were standard equipment; gear to protect the fragile human form until the lower oxygen-rich regions of the air ocean could be reached in event of trouble. But the Aztec was an all-or-nothing affair. There were no escape provisions, no ejection seats, for ejection would be impossible at the rocket's speeds during its critical climb through the atmosphere. Either everything went according to the book or . . . or else, he concluded grimly. But it had one good aspect. Aside from the heavy safety harnessing, he would be free of the intolerably clumsy suit until moonfall. If anything went wrong, well . . .

He bit the thought off, feeling the tension building inside him. He had never considered himself the hero type. He had prided himself that his ability to handle hot planes was a reflection of his competence rather than courage. Courage, to him, meant capable performance in the face of fear. He had never known fear in any type of aircraft, hence never before had courage been a requisite of his job. It was that simple to him. His thorough knowledge of the Aztec's theoretical flight characteristics had given him extreme confidence, thus the feeling of tension was distracting. He held his hand out. It seemed steady enough.

Prochaska caught the gesture and said, "I'm a little shaky myself."

Crag grinned. "They tell me the first thousand miles are the hardest."

"Amen. After that I won't worry."

The countdown had begun. Crag looked out the side port. Tiny figures were withdrawing from the base of the rocket. The engine of a fuel truck sounded faintly, then died away. Everything seemed unhurried, routine. He found himself admiring the men who went so matter-of-factly about the job of hurling a rocket into the gulfs between planets. Once, during his indoctrination, he had watched a Thor firing . . . had seen the missile climb into the sky, building up to orbital speed. Its launchers had been the same sort of men—unhurried, methodical, checking the minutiae that went into such an effort. Only this time there was a difference. The missile contained men.

Off to one side he saw the launch crew moving into an instrumented dugout. Colonel Gotch would be there, puffing on his pipe, his face expressionless, watching the work of many years come to . . . what?

He looked around the cabin for the hundredth time. Larkwell and Nagel were strapped in their seats, backs horizontal to the floor, looking up at him. The tremendous forces of acceleration applied at right angles to the spine—transverse g—was far more tolerable than in any other position. Or so the space medicine men said. He hoped they were right, that in this position the body could withstand the hell ahead. He gave a last look at the two men behind him. Larkwell wore an owlish expression. His teeth were clamped tight, cording his jaws. Nagel's face was intent, its lines rigid. It gave Crag the odd impression of an alabaster sculpture. Prochaska, who occupied the seat next to him facing the control panels, was testing his safety belts.

Crag gave him a quick sidelong glance. Prochaska's job

was in many respects as difficult as his own. Perhaps more so. The sallow-faced electronics chief bore the responsibility of monitoring the drones—shepherding, first Drone Able, then its sisters to follow—across the vacuum gulfs and, finally, into Arzachel, a pinpoint cavity in the rocky wastelands of the moon. In addition, he was charged with monitoring, repairing and installing all the communication and electronic equipment, no small job in itself. Yes, a lot depended on the almost fragile man sitting alongside him. He looked at his own harnessing, testing its fit.

Colonel Gotch came on the communicator. "Pickering's in orbit," he said briefly. "No details yet."

Crag sighed in relief. Somehow Pickering's success augured well for their own attempt. He gave a last check of the communication gear. The main speaker was set just above the instrument panel, between him and Prochaska. In addition, both he and the Chief—the title he had conferred on Prochaska as his special assistant—were supplied with insert earphones and lip microphones for use during high noise spectrums, or when privacy was desired. Crag, as Commander, could limit all communications to his own personal headgear by merely flipping a switch. Gotch had been the architect of that one. He was a man who like private lines.

"Five minutes to zero, Commander."

Commander! Crag liked that. He struggled against his harnessing to glance back over his shoulder. Nagel's body, scrunched deep into his bucket seat, seemed pitifully thin under the heavy harnessing. His face was bloodless, taut. Crag momentarily wondered what strange course of events had brought him to the rocket. He didn't look like Crag's picture of a spaceman. Not at all. But then, none of them looked like supermen. Still, courage wasn't a matter of looks, he told himself. It was a matter of action.

He swiveled his head around farther. Larkwell reclined next to Nagel with eyes closed. Only the fast rise and fall of his chest told of his inner tensions—that and the hawk-like grip of his fingers around the arm rests. Worried, Crag thought. But we're all worried. He cast a sidelong glance at Prochaska. The man's face held enormous calm. He reached over and picked up the console mike, then sat for what seemed an eternity before the countdown reached minus one minute. He plugged in his ear-insert microphone.

"Thirty seconds . . ." The voice over the speaker boomed. Prochaska suddenly became busy checking his instruments. Jittery despite his seeming calm, Crag thought.

"Twenty seconds . . ." He caught himself checking his controls, as if he could gain some last moment's knowledge from the banks of levers and dials and knobs.

"Ten . . . nine . . . eight . . ." He experimentally pulled at his harnessing, feeling somewhat hypnotized by the magic of the numbers coming over the communicator.

"Three . . . two . . ."

Crag said, "Ready on one."

He punched a button. A muted roar drifted up from the stern. He listened for a moment. Satisfied, he moved the cut-in switch. The roar increased, becoming almost deafening in the cabin despite its soundproofing. He tested the radio and steering rockets and gave a last sidelong glance at Prochaska. The Chief winked. The act made him feel better. I should be nervous, he thought, or just plain damned scared. But things were happening too fast. He adjusted his lip mike and reached for the controls, studying his hand as he did so. Still steady. He stirred the controls a bit and the roar became hellish. He chewed his lip and took a deep breath, exhaling slowly.

He said, "Off to the moon."

Prochaska nodded. Crag moved the controls. The cabin seemed to bob, wobble, vibrate. A high hum came from somewhere. He glanced downward through the side port. The Aztec seemed to be hanging in mid-air just above the desert floor. Off to one side he could see the concrete controls dugout. The tiny figures had vanished.

He thought: *Gotch is sweating it out now.* In the past rockets had burned on the pad . . . blown up in mid-air . . . plunged off course and had to be destroyed. The idea brought his head up with a snap. Was there a safety officer down there with a finger on a button . . . prepared to destroy the Aztec if it wavered in flight?

He cut the thought off and moved the main power switch, bringing the control full over. The ship bucked, and the desert dropped away with a suddenness that brought a siege of nausea. He tightened his stomach muscles like the space medicine doctors had instructed.

The first moment was bad. There was unbelievable thunder, a fraction of a second when his brain seemed to blank, a quick surge of fear. Up . . . up. The Aztec's rate of acceleration climbed sharply. At a prescribed point in time the nose of the rocket moved slightly toward the east. It climbed at an impossibly steep slant, rushing up from the earth. Crag swept his eyes over the banks of instruments, noted the positions of the controls, tried to follow what the faint voice in his earphone was telling him. Dials with wavering needles . . . knobs with blurry numerals . . . a cacophony of noise, light and movement—all this and more was crowded into seconds.

The rocket hurtled upward, driven by the tidal kinetic energy generated by the combustion of high velocity exhaust, born in an inferno of thousands of degrees. Behind him giant thrust chambers hungrily consumed the volatile fuel, spewing the high-pressure gases forth at more than nine thousand miles per hour. The crushing increased, driving him against the back of his seat. His heart began laboring . . . became a sledge hammer inside his chest wall.

He lost all sense of motion. Only the almost unendurable weight crushing his body downward mattered. He managed a glimpse of the desert through the side port. It lay far below, its salient details erased. The roar of the giant motors became muted. There was a singing in his ears, a high whine he didn't like.

The Aztec began to tilt, falling off to the right.

He cast a quick glance at the engine instruments. A red light blinked. Number three was delivering slightly less thrust than the others. Somewhere in the complex of machinery a mechanical sensing device reacted. Engines one and two were throttled back and the rocket straightened. A second device shifted the mix on engine three, bringing thrust into balance. All three engines resumed full power.

"Twenty-five thousand feet," Prochaska chattered. His voice was tinny over the small insert earphone provided for communications, especially for those first few hellish moments when the whole universe seemed collapsed into one huge noise spectrum. Noise and pressure.

"Forty-five thousand . . ."

They were moving up fast now—three g, four g, five g. Crag's body weight was equal to 680 pounds. The dense reaches of the troposphere—the weather belt where storms are born—dropped below them. They hurtled through the rarefied, bitterly cold and utterly calm stratosphere.

"Eighty thousand feet . . ."

Crag struggled to move his body. His hand was leaden on the controls, as if all life had been choked from it. A hot metal ball filled his chest. He couldn't breathe. Panic . . . until he remembered to breathe at the top of his lungs.

At eighteen miles a gale of wind drove west. Rudders on the Aztec compensated, she leaned slightly into the blast, negating its drift. The winds ceased . . . rudders shifted . . . the rocket slanted skyward. Faster . . . faster.

Prochaska called off altitudes almost continuously, the chattering gone from his voice. Crag was still struggling against the pinning weight when it decreased, vanished. The firestream from the tail pipe gave a burst of smoke and died. *Brennschluss*—burnout.

The Aztec hurtled toward the cosmic-ray laden ionosphere, driven only by the inertial forces generated in the now silent thrust chambers. The hard components of cosmic rays —fast mesons, high energy protons and neutrons—would rip through the ship. *If dogs and monkeys can take it, so can man.* That's what Gotch had said. He hoped Gotch was right. Somewhere, now, the first stage would fall away. It would follow them, at ever greater distances, until finally its trajectory would send it plunging homeward.

"Cut in." Prochaska's voice was a loud boom in the silence. A strident voice from the communicator was trying to tell them they were right on the button. Crag moved a second switch. The resultant acceleration drove him against the back of his seat, violently expelling the air from his lungs. He fought against the increasing gravities, conscious of pressure and noise in his ears; pressure and noise mixed with fragments of voice. His lips pulled tight against his teeth. The thudding was his heart. He tightened his stomach muscles, trying to ease the weight on his chest. A mighty hand was gripped around his lungs, squeezing out the air. But it wasn't as bad as the first time. They were piercing the thermosphere where the outside temperature gradient would zoom upward toward the 2,000 degree mark.

Prochaska spoke matter-of-factly into his lip mike, "Fifty miles."

Crag marveled at his control . . . his calm. No, he didn't have to worry about the Chief. The little runt had it. Crag tried to grin. The effort was a pain.

The Aztec gave a lurch, altering the direction of forces on their bodies again as a servo control kicked the ship into the long shallow spiral of escape. It moved upward and more easterly, its nose slanted toward the stars, seeking its new course. Crag became momentarily dizzy. His vision blurred

. . . the instrument panel became a kaleidoscope of dancing, merging patterns. Then it was past, all except the three g force nailing him to the seat.

He spoke into the communicator. "How we doing?"

"Fine, Commander, just fine," Gotch rasped. "The toughest part's over."

Over like hell, Crag thought. A one-way rocket to the moon and he tells me the toughest part's over. Lord, I should work in a drugstore!

"Seventy-five miles and two hundred miles east," the Chief intoned. Crag made a visual instrument check. Everything looked okay. No red lights. Just greens. Wonderful greens that meant everything was hunky-dory. He liked green. He wanted to see how Larkwell and Nagel were making out but couldn't turn his head. It's rougher on them, he thought. They can't see the instruments, can't hear the small voice from Alpine. They just have to sit and take it. Sit and feel the unearthly pressures and weights and hope everything's okay.

"Ninety-six miles . . . speed 3.1 miles per second," Prochaska chanted a short while later.

It's as easy as that, Crag thought. Years and years of planning and training; then you just step in and go. Not that they were there yet. He remembered the rockets that had burned . . . exploded . . . the drifting hulks that still orbited around the earth. No, it wasn't over yet. Not by a long shot.

The quiet came again. The earth, seen through the side port, seemed tremendously far away. It was a study in greens and yellow-browns and whitish ragged areas where the eye was blocked by cloud formations. Straight out the sky was black, starry. Prochaska reached up and swung the glare shield over the forward port. The sun, looked at even indirectly, was a blinding orb, intolerable to the unprotected eye. Night above . . . day below. A sun that blazed without breaking the ebon skies. Strange, Crag mused. He had been prepared for this, prepared by long hours of instruction. But now, confronted with a day that was night, he could only wonder. For a moment he felt small, insignificant, and wondered at brazen man. Who dared come here? I dared, he thought. A feeling of pride grew within him. I dared. The stars are mine. . . .

Stage three was easy by comparison. It began with the muted roar of thrust chambers almost behind them, a noise spectrum almost solely confined to the interior of the rocket. Outside there was no longer sufficient air molecules to convey even a whisper of sound. Nor was there a pressure build-up. The stage three engine was designed for extremely low thrust extended over a correspondingly longer time. It would drive them through the escape spiral—an orbital path around the earth during which time they would slowly increase both altitude and speed.

Crag's body felt light; not total weightlessness, but extremely light. His instruments told him they were breaching the exosphere, where molecular matter had almost ceased to exist. The atoms of the exosphere were lonely, uncrowded, isolated particles. It was the top of the air ocean where, heretofore, only monkeys, dogs and smaller test animals had gone. It was the realm of Sputniks . . . Explorers . . . Vanguards—all the test rockets which had made the Aztec possible. They still sped their silent orbits, borne on the space tides of velocity; eternal tombs of dogs and monkeys. And after monkey—man.

The communicator gave a burp. A voice came through the static. Drone Able was aloft. It had blasted off from its blasting pad at Burning Sands just moments after the Aztec. Prochaska bent over the radarscope and fiddled with some knobs. The tube glowed and dimmed, then it was there—a tiny pip.

Alpine came in with more data. They watched its course. Somewhere far below them and hundreds of miles to the west human minds were guiding the drone by telemeter control, vectoring it through space to meet the Aztec. It was, Crag thought, applied mathematics. He marveled at the science which enabled them to do it. One moment the drone was just a pip on the scope, climbing up from the sere earth, riding a firestream to the skies; the next it was tons of metal scorching through space, cutting into their flight path—a giant screaming up from its cradle..

It was Prochaska's turn to sweat. The job of taking it over was his. He bent over his instruments, ears tuned to the communicator fingers nervous on the drone controls. The drone hurtled toward them at a frightening speed.

Crag kept his fingers on the steering controls just in case, his mind following the Chief's hands. They began moving more certainly. Prochaska tossed his head impatiently, bending lower over the instrument console. Crag strained against his harnessing to see out of the side port. The drone was visible now, a silver shaft growing larger with appalling rapidity. A thin skein of vapor trailed from its trail, fluffing into nothingness.

If angle of closure remains constant, you're on collision course. The words from the Flying Safety Manual popped into his mind. He studied the drone.

Angle of closure was constant!

Crag hesitated. Even a touch on the steering rockets could be bad. Very bad. The slightest change in course at their present speed would impose tremendous g forces on their bodies, perhaps greater than they could stand. He looked at the Chief and licked his lips. The man was intent on his instruments, seemingly lost to the world. His fingers had ceased all random movement. Every motion had precise meaning. He was hooked onto Drone Able's steering rockets now, manipulating the controls with extreme precision. He was a concert pianist playing the strident music of space, an overture written in metal and flaming gas. Tiny corrections occurred in the Drone's flight path.

"Got her lined up," Prochaska announced without moving his eyes from the scope. He gradually narrowed the distance between the rockets until they were hurtling through space on parallel courses scant miles apart. He gave a final check and looked at Crag. They simultaneously emitted big sighs.

"Had me worried for a moment," Crag confessed.

"Me, too." The Chief looked out of the side port. "Man, it looks like a battle wagon."

Crag squinted through the port. Drone Able was a silver bullet in space, a twin of the Aztec except in color. A drone with view ports. He smiled thoughtfully. Every exterior of the drone had been planned to make it appear like a manned vehicle. Gotch was the architect of that bit of deception, he thought. The Colonel hadn't missed a bet.

He looked at the earth. It was a behemoth in space; a huge curved surface falling away in all directions; a mosaic of grays punctuated by swaths of blue-green tints and splotches of white where fleecy clouds rode the top of the troposphere. His momentary elation vanished, replaced by an odd depression. The world was far away, retreating into the cosmic mists. The aftermath, he thought. A chill presentiment crept into his mind—a premonition of impending disaster.

CHAPTER 4

THE COMMUNICATOR came to life with data on Pickering The satelloid was moving higher, faster than the Aztec, riding the rim of the exosphere where the atmosphere is indistinguishable from absolute space. Crag felt thankful he hadn't been tabbed for the job. The satelloid was a fragile thing compared to the Aztec—a moth compared to a hawk. It was a relative handful of light metals and delicate electronic components, yet it moved at frightful speeds over the course the armchair astronauts had dubbed "Sputnik Avenue." It was a piloted vehicle, a mite with small stubby wings to enable it to glide through the air ocean to safe sanctuary after orbiting the earth. Pickering would be crouched in its scant belly, a space hardly larger than his body, cramped in a pressure suit that made movement all but impossible. His smallest misjudgment would spell instant death. Crag marveled at Pickering's audacity. Clearly he had the roughest mission. While he thought about it, he kept one part of his mind centered on the communicator absorbing the data on the satelloid's position and speed.

The Northern tip of Africa came up fast. The Dark Continent of history seen from the borders of space was a yellow-green splotch hemmed by blue. The satelloid was still beyond the Aztec's radar range but a data link analog painted in the relationship between the two space vehicles. The instrument's automatic grid measured the distance between them in hundreds of miles. Pickering, aloft before them, had fled into the east and already was beginning to overtake them from the west. The ships were seen on the analog as two pips, two mites aloft in the air ocean. Crag marveled at the satelloid's tremendous speed. It was a ray of metal flashing along the fringes of space, a rapier coming out of the west.

The Middle East passed under them, receding, a mass of yellow-green and occasional smoke-blue splotches. The earth was a giant curvature, not yet an orb, passing into the shadow of night. It was a night of fantastic shortness, broken by daylight over the Pacific. The ocean was an incredible blue,

blue-black he decided. The harsh sound of the communicator came to life. Someone wanted a confab with Crag. A private confab. Prochaska wrinkled his brow questioningly. Crag switched to his ear insert phone and acknowledged.

"A moment," a voice said. He waited.

"Commander, we've bad news for you." It was Gotch's voice, a rasp coming over a great distance.

"The S-two reports a rocket being tracked by radar. ComSoPac's picked it up. It's on intercept course."

Crag's thoughts raced. The S-two was the satelloid's code name. "Any idea what kind?"

"Probably a sub-launched missile—riding a beam right to you. Or the drone," he added. He was silent for a second. "Well, we sort of expected this might happen, Commander. It's a tough complication."

A helluva lot of good that does, Crag thought. What next? Another set of pilots, more indoctrination, new rockets, another zero hour. Gotch would win the moon if he had to use the whole Air Force. He said, "Well, it's been a nice trip, so far."

"Get Prochaska on the scope."

"He's on and . . . hold it." The Chief was making motions toward the scope. "No, it's the satelloid. He's—"

Gotch broke in with more data. Then it was there.

"He's got it," Crag announced. Gotch was silent. He watched the analog. All three pips were visible. The satelloid was still above them, rushing in, fast. The interceptor was lower to the northwest, cutting into their path. He thought it was the Drone Able story all over again. Only this time it wasn't a supply rocket. It was a warhead, a situation they couldn't control.

Couldn't control? Or could they? He debated the question, then quickly briefed Prochaska and cut him in on the com circuit.

"We can use Drone Able as an intercept," he told Gotch.

"No!" The word came explosively.

Crag snapped, "Drone Able won't be a damn bit of good without the Aztec."

"No, this is ground control, Commander." Gotch abruptly cut off. Crag cursed.

"Calling Step One . . . Calling Step One. S-two calling Step One. Are you receiving? Over." The voice came faint over the communicator, rising and falling.

"Step One," Crag said, adjusting his lip mike. He acknowledged the code call while his mind registered the fact it wasn't Alpine Base. There was a burst of static. He waited a moment, puzzled.

"S-two calling . . ."

Pickering! He had been slow in recognizing the satelloid's code call. The voice faded—was lost. His thought raced. Pickering was up there in the satelloid moving higher, faster than the Aztec, hurtling along the rim of space in a great circle around the earth. The stubby-winged rocket ship was a minute particle in infinity, yet it represented a part in the great adventure. It was the hand of Michael Gotch reaching toward them. For the instant, the knowledge gave him a ray of hope—hope as quickly dashed. The S-two was just a high-speed observation and relay platform; a manned vehicle traveling the communication orbit established by the Army's earlier Explorer missiles. He turned back to Prochaska and sketched in his plan of using Drone Able as an intercept.

"Could be." The Chief bit his lip reflectively. "We could control her through her steering rockets, but we'd have to be plenty sharp. We'd only get one crack."

"Chances are the intercept is working on a proximity fuse," Crag reasoned. "All we'd have to do is work the drone into its flight path. We could use our own steering rockets to give us a bigger margin of safety."

"What would the loss of Able mean?"

Crag shrugged. "I'm more concerned with what the loss of the Aztec would mean."

"Might work." The Chief looked sharply at him. "What does Alpine say?"

"They say nuts." Crag looked at the scope. The intercept was much nearer. So was the S-two. Pickering's probably coming in for an eye-witness report, he thought sourly. Probably got an automatic camera so Gotch can watch the show. He looked quizzically at Prochaska. The Chief wore a frozen mask. He got back on the communicator and repeated his request. When he finished, there was a dead silence in the void.

The Colonel's answer was unprintable. He looked thoughtfully at Prochaska. Last time he'd broken ground orders he'd been invited to leave the Air Force. But Gotch had taken him despite that. He glanced over his shoulder trying to formulate a plan. Larkwell was lying back in his seat, eyes closed. Lucky dog, he thought. He doesn't know what he's in for. He twisted his head further. Nagel watched him with a narrow look. He pushed the oxygen man from his mind and turned back to the analog. The pip that was Pickering had moved a long way across the grid. The altitude needle tied into the grid showed that the satelloid was dropping fast. The intercept was nearer, too. Much nearer. Prochaska watched the scene on his radarscope.

"She's coming fast," he murmured. His face had paled.

"Too fast," Crag gritted. He got on the communicator and called Alpine. Gotch came on immediately.

Crag said defiantly. "We're going to use Drone Able as an intercept. It's the only chance."

"Commander, I ordered ground control." The Colonel's voice was icy, biting.

"Ground has no control over this situation," Crag snapped angrily.

"I said ground control, Commander. That's final."

"I'm using Drone Able."

"Commander Crag, you'll wind up cleaning the heads at Alpine," Gotch raged. "Don't move that Drone."

For a moment the situation struck him as humorous. Just now he'd like to be guaranteed the chance to clear the heads at Alpine Base. It sounded good—real good. There was another burst of static. Pickering's voice came in—louder, clearer, a snap through the ether.

"Don't sacrifice the drone, Commander!"

"Do you know a better way?"

Pickering's voice dropped to a laconic drawl.

"Reckon so."

Crag glanced at the analog and gave a visible start. The satelloid was lower, moving in faster along a course which would take it obliquely through the space path being traversed by the Aztec. If there was such a thing as a wake in space, that's where the satelloid would chop through, cutting down toward the intercept. He's using his power, he thought, the scant amount of fuel he would need for landing. But if he used it up . . .

He slashed the thought off and swung to the communicator.

"Step One to S-two . . . Step One to S-two . . ."

"S-two." Pickering came in immediately.

Crag barked, "You can't—"

"That's my job," Pickering cut in. "You gotta get that bucket to the moon." Crag looked thoughtfully at the communicator.

"Okay," he said finally. "Thanks, fellow."

"Don't mention it. The Air Force is always ready to serve," Pickering said. "Adios." He cut off.

Crag stared at the analog, biting his lip, feeling the emotion surge inside him. It grew to a tumult.

"Skipper!" Prochaska's voice was startled. "For God's sake . . . look!"

Crag swung his eyes to the scope. The blip representing

Pickering had cut their flight path, slicing obliquely through their wake. At its tremendous speed only the almost total absence of air molecules kept the satelloid from turning into a blazing torch. Down . . . down . . . plunging to meet the death roaring up from the Pacific. They followed it silently. A brief flare showed on the scope. They looked at the screen for a long moment.

"He was a brave man," Prochaska said simply.

"A pile of guts." Crag got on the communicator. Gotch listened. When he had finished, Gotch said:

"After this, Commander, follow ground orders. You damned near fouled up the works. I don't want to see that happen again."

"Yes, Sir, but I couldn't have expected that move."

"What do you think Pickering was up there for?" Gotch asked softly. "He knew what he was doing. That was his job. Just like the couple that got bumped at the Blue Door. It's tough, Commander, but some people have to die. A lot have, already, and there'll be a lot more."

He added brusquely, "You'll get your chance." The communicator was silent for a moment. "Well, carry on."

"Aye, aye, Sir," Crag said. He glanced over his shoulder.

Larkwell was leaning over in his seat, twisting his body to see out the side port. His face was filled with the wonder of space. Nagel didn't stir. His eyes were big saucers in his white, thin face. Crag half expected to see his lips quiver, and wondered briefly at the courage it must have taken for him to volunteer. He didn't seem at all like the hero type. Still, look at Napoleon. You could never tell what a man had until the chips were down. Well, the chips *were* down. Nagel better have it. He turned reflectively back to the forward port thinking that the next two days would be humdrum. Nothing would ever seem tough again. Not after what they had just been through.

Prochaska fell into the routine of calling out altitude and

speed. Crag listened with one part of his mind occupied with Pickering's sacrifice. Would he have had the courage to drive the satelloid into the warhead? Did it take more guts to do that than to double for a man slated to be murdered? He mulled the questions. Plainly, Step One was jammed with heroes.

"Altitude, 1,000 miles, speed, 22,300." Prochaska whispered the words, awe in his voice. They looked at each other wordlessly.

"We've made it," Crag exulted. "We're on that old moon trajectory." The Chief's face reflected his wonder. Crag studied his instruments. Speed slightly over 22,300 miles per hour. The radar altimeter showed the Aztec slightly more than one thousand miles above the earth's surface. He hesitated, then cut off the third stage engine. The fuel gauge indicated a bare few gallons left. This small amount, he knew, represented error in the precise computations of escape. Well, the extra weight was negligible. At the same time, they couldn't afford added acceleration. He became aware that the last vestige of weight had vanished. He moved his hand. No effort. No effort at all. Space, he thought, the first successful manned space ship.

Elation swept him. He, Adam Crag, was in space. Not just the top of the atmosphere but absolute space—the big vacuum that surrounded the world. This had been the aim . . . the dream . . . the goal. And so quick!

He flicked his mind back. It seemed almost no time at all since the Germans had electrified the world with the V-2, a primitive rocket that scarcely reached seventy miles above the earth, creeping at a mere 3,000 miles per hour.

The Americans had strapped a second stage to the German prototype, creating the two-stage V-2-Wac Corporal and sending it 250 miles into the tall blue at speeds better than 5,000 miles per hour. It had been a battle even then, he thought, remembering the dark day the Russians beat the

West with Sputnik I . . . seemingly demolished it with Sputnik II—until the U. S. Army came through with Explorer I. That had been the real beginning. IRBM's and ICBM's had been born. Missiles and counter-missiles. Dogs, monkeys and mice had ridden the fringes of space. But never man.

A deep sense of satisfaction flooded him. The Aztec had been the first. The Aztec under Commander Adam Crag. The full sense of the accomplishment was just beginning to strike him. We've beaten the enemy, he thought. We've won. It had been a grim battle waged on a technological front; a battle between nations in which, ironically, each victory by either side took mankind a step nearer emancipation from the world. Man could look forward now, to a bright shiny path leading to the stars. This was the final step. The Big Step. The step that would tie together two worlds. In a few short days the Aztec would reach her lonely destination, Arzachel, a bleak spot in the universe. Adam Crag, the Man in the Moon. He hoped. He turned toward the others, trying to wipe the smug look from his face.

The oddity of weightlessness was totally unlike anything he had expected despite the fact its symptoms had been carefully explained during the indoctrination program. He was sitting in the pilot's seat, yet he wasn't. He felt no sense of pressure against the seat, or against anything else, for that matter. It was, he thought, like sitting on air, as light as a mote of dust drifting in a breeze. Sure, he'd experienced weightlessness before, when pushing a research stratojet through a high-speed trajectory to counter the pull of gravity, for example. But those occasions had lasted only brief moments. He moved his hand experimentally upward—a move that ended like the strike of a snake. Yeah, it was going to take some doing to learn control of his movements. He looked at Prochaska. The Chief was feeding data to Alpine Base. He finished and grinned broadly at Crag. His eyes were elated.

"Sort of startling, isn't it?"

"Amen," Crag agreed. "I'm almost afraid to loosen my harnessing."

"Alpine says we're right on the button—schedule, course and speed. There's a gal operator on now."

"That's good. That means we're back to routine." Crag loosened his harnesses and twisted around in his seat. Larkwell was moving his hands experimentally. He saw Crag and grinned foolishly. Nagel looked ill. His face was pinched, bloodless, his eyes red-rimmed. He caught Crag's look and nodded, without expression.

"Pretty rough," Crag said sympathetically. His voice, in the new-born silence, possessed a curious muffled effect. "We're past the worst."

Nagel's lips twisted derisively. "Yeah?"

The querulous tone grated Crag and he turned back to the controls. *Every minor irritant will assume major proportions.* That's what Doc Weldon had warned. Well, damnit, he wouldn't let Nagel get him down. Besides, what was his gripe? They were all in the same boat. He turned to the instrument console, checking the myriad of dials, gauges and scopes. Everything seemed normal, if there was such a thing as normalcy in space. He said reflectively, speaking to no one in particular:

"Maybe I should have been more truthful with the Colonel before taking on this damned job of moon pilot. There's something I didn't tell him."

"What?" Prochaska's face was startled.

"I've never been to the moon before."

CHAPTER 5

"ALPINE wants a private confab," Prochaska said. His voice was ominous. "Probably another stinker."

"Again?" Crag plugged in his ear insert microphone thinking he wasn't going to like what he'd hear. Just when things had started looking smooth too. He cut Prochaska out of the system and acknowledged.

"Crag?" Gotch's voice was brittle, hard. He looked sideways at Prochaska, who was studiously examining one of the instruments, trying to give him the privacy demanded. He shifted his head. Larkwell was standing at the side port with his back toward him. Nagel lay back in his seat, eyes closed.

Crag answered softly. "Shoot."

"More bad news," Gotch reported somberly. "Burning Sands picked a package out of Drone Able just before launch time. It's just been identified."

"Check," he replied, trying to assimilate what Gotch was telling him.

Gotch stated flatly. "It was a time bomb. Here's a description. Bomb was packaged in a flat black plastic case about one by four inches. Probably not big enough to wreck the drone but big enough to destroy the controls. It was found tucked in the wiring of the main panel. Got that?"

"Check."

"The bomb squad hasn't come through with full details yet. If you find a mate, don't try to disarm it. Dump it, pronto!"

"Can't. It'll stay with us."

"It's size indicates it wouldn't be fatal if it exploded outside the hull," Gotch rasped. "It was designed to wreck controls. If you find one, dump it. That's an order." The

FIRST ON THE MOON 47

earphones were silent. Crag was swiveling toward Prochaska when they came to life again.

"One other thing." Gotch was silent for a moment. Crag pictured him carefully framing his words. "It means that the situation is worse than we thought," he said finally.

"They haven't left anything to chance. If you have a bomb, it was carried there after the final security check. Do you follow me?"

"Yeah," Crag answered thoughtfully. He sat for a moment, debating what to do. Prochaska didn't ask any questions. Gotch was telling him that the Aztec might be mined. Wait, what else had he said? *The bomb was carried there after the security check.* That spelled traitor. The Aztec had been shaken down too often and too thoroughly for Intelligence to have muffed. It would have to have been planted at the last moment. If there was a bomb. He'd better keep quiet until Gotch's suspicions were proven false—or verified.

He turned toward Prochaska, keeping his voice low. "Search the console panels—every inch of them."

He looked around. Nagel and Larkwell were back in their seats. Nagel seemed asleep, but Larkwell's face was speculative. Crag's eyes swept the cabin. Spare oxygen tanks, packaged pressure suits, water vents, chemical commode, the algae chamber and spare chemicals to absorb carbon dioxide in case the algae system failed—these and more items filled every wall, cupboard, occupied every cubic inch of space beyond the bare room needed for human movement. Where was the most sensitive spot? The controls. He sighed and turned back to the panels.

Prochaska was methodically running his hands through the complex of wiring under the instrument panels. His face was a question, the face of a man who didn't know what he was looking for. He decided not to tell him . . . yet. His earphones gave a burst of static followed by the Colonel's hurried voice.

"Burning Sands reports packaged timed for 0815," he snapped. "That's eight minutes away. Get on the ball. If you've got one there, it's probably a twin."

"Okay," Crag acknowledged. "Adios, we've got work to do." He swung toward Nagel.

"Break out the pressure suits," he barked. "Lend him a hand, Larkwell."

Nagel's eyes opened. "Pressure suits?"

"Check. We may need them in a couple of minutes."

"But—"

"Get to it," Crag rasped. "It may be a matter of life or death." He turned. Prochaska was still examining the wiring. No time to search the rest of the cabin, he thought. It might be anywhere. It would have to be the panels or nothing. Besides, that was the most logical place. He went to the Chief's assistance, searching the panels on his side of the board, pushing his fingers gently between the maze of wiring. Nothing below the analog, the engine instruments, the radar altimeter. He glanced at the chronometer and began to sweat. The hands on the dial seemed to be racing. Prochaska finished his side of the console and looked sideways at him. Better tell him, Crag thought.

He said calmly. "Time bomb. Burning Sands says, if we have one, it may blow in—" he glanced hurriedly at the chronometer—"five minutes."

Prochaska looked hurriedly at the array of gear lining the bulkheads.

"Probably in the controls, if we have one." Crag finished the panels on his side without any luck. Prochaska hastily started re-examining the wiring. Crag followed after him. A moment later his fingers found it, a smooth flat case deeply imbedded between the wiring. Prochaska had gone over that panel a moment before! The thought struck him even as he moved it out, handling it gingerly. Prochaska showed his surprise. Crag glanced at Nagel and Larkwell. They had the

FIRST ON THE MOON

49

suits free. He laid the bomb on the console. Larkwell saw it. His face showed understanding. He heaved one of the suits to Prochaska and a second one to Crag. They hurriedly donned them. Space limitations made it an awkward task. Crag kept his eyes on the chronometer. The hand seemed to whiz across the dial. He began to sweat, conscious that he was breathing heavily.

"Short exposure," he rapped out. "Minimum pressure." He slipped on his helmet, secured it to the neck ring and snapped on the face plate. He turned the oxygen valve and felt the pressure build up within the suit and helmet. The chronometer showed two minutes to go. He snapped a glance around. Nagel peered at him through his thick face plate with a worried expression. Larkwell's lips were compressed against his teeth. His jaws worked spasmodically. Both were waiting, tense, watching him.

Prochaska was the last to finish. Crag waited impatiently for him to switch on his oxygen valve before picking up the bomb. He motioned the others to stand back and began opening the dogs which secured the escape hatch. He hesitated on the last one. The escaping air could whisk him into space in a flash. The same thing had happened to crewmen riding in bubbles that broke at high altitude. Whoosh! He'd be gone! Conceivably, it could suck the cabin clean. Fortunately their gear had been secured as protection against the high g forces of escape. Too late to lash himself with the seat harnessing. Time was running out. Panic touched his mind. Calm down, Crag, he told himself. Play it cool, boy.

Prochaska saw his dilemma at the same instant. He squatted on the deck and thrust his legs straight out from the hips, straddling one of the seat supports. Larkwell and Nagel hurriedly followed suit. Crag cast a backward glance at the chronometer—a minute and ten seconds to go! He threw himself to one side of the hatch, squatted and hooked an arm into a panel console, hoping it was strong enough.

He laid the bomb on the deck next to the hatch and reached up with his free hand, held his breath, hesitated, and jarred the last dog loose.

The hatch exploded open. A giant claw seemed to grab his body, pulling him toward the opening. It passed as quickly as it came, leaving him weak, breathless. The bomb had been whisked into space. He got to his feet and grasped the hatch combing, looking out. It was a giddy, vertiginous moment. Before him yawned a great purple-black maw, a blacker purple than that seen through the view ports. It was studded with unbelievably brilliant stars agleam with the hard luster of diamonds—white diamonds and blue sapphires.

Something bright blinked in space.

He hesitated. The cold was already coming through his suit. He remembered he hadn't turned on either the heating element or interphone system. He drew the hatch shut and dogged it down, then switched both on. The others saw his movements and followed suit.

"See anything?" Prochaska was the first to ask. His voice sounded tinny and far away. Crag adjusted his amplifier and said grimly:

"It blew."

"How . . . how did it get here?" He identified the voice as Nagel's.

He snapped brusquely, "That's what I'm going to find out." Larkwell was silent. Nagel began fiddling with the oxygen valves. They waited, quietly, each absorbed in his thoughts until Nagel indicated it was safe to remove their suits. Crag's thoughts raced while he shucked the heavy garments. It's past, he thought, but the saboteur's still here. Who? He flicked his eyes over the men. Who? That's what he had to find out—soon! When the suit was off, he hurriedly put through a call to Gotch, reporting what had happened.

The Colonel listened without comment. When Crag finished, he was silent for a moment. Finally he replied:

"Here's where we stand. We will immediately comb the record of every intelligence agent involved in the last shakedown. We'll also recomb the records of the Aztec crew, including yours. I've got to tell you this because it's serious. If there's a saboteur aboard—and I think there is—then the whole operation's in jeopardy. It'll be up to you to keep your eyes open and analyze your men. We've tried to be careful. We've checked everyone involved back to birth. But there's always the sleeper. It's happened before."

"Check," Crag said. "I only hope you don't catch up with all my early peccadillos."

"This is no time to be funny. Now, some more news for you. Washington reports that the enemy launched another missile this morning."

"Another one?" Crag sighed softly. This time there would be no satelloid, no Pickering to give his life.

The Colonel continued grimly. "Radar indicates this is a different kind of rocket. Its rate of climb . . . its trajectory . . . indicates it's manned. Now it's a race."

Crag thought a moment. "Any sign of a drone with it?"

"No, that's the surprising part, if this is a full-scale attempt at establishing a moon base. And we believe it is."

Crag asked sharply. "It couldn't be their atom-powered job?" The possibility filled him with alarm.

"Positively not. We've got our finger squarely on that one and it's a good year from launch-date. No, this is a conventional rocket . . . perhaps more advanced than we had believed . . ." His voice dropped off. "We'll keep you posted," he added after a minute.

"Roger." Crag sighed. He removed the earphone reflectively. He wouldn't tell the others yet. Now that they were in space maybe . . . just maybe . . . he could find time to catch his breath. Damn, they hadn't anticipated all this during indoctrination. The intercept-missile . . . time bomb . . . possible traitor in the crew. What more could go wrong? For just a second he felt an intense hostility toward Gotch. An Air Force full of pilots and he had to pick him —and he wasn't even in the Air Force at the time. Lord, he should have contented himself with jockeying a jet airliner on some nice quiet hop. Like between L. A. and Pearl . . . with a girl at each end of the run.

He thought wistfully about the prospect while he made a routine check of the instruments. Cabin pressure normal . . . temperature 78 degrees F. . . . nothing alarming in the radiation and meteor impact readings. Carbon dioxide content normal. Things might get routine after all, he thought moodily. Except for one thing. The new rocket flashing skyward from east of the Caspian. One thing he was sure of. It spelled trouble.

CHAPTER 6

THE U. S. NAVY's Space Scan Radar Station No. 5 picked up the new rocket before it was fairly into space. It clung to it with an electromagnetic train, bleeding it of data. The information was fed into computers, digested, analyzed and transferred to Alpine Base, and thence telemetered to the Aztec where it appeared as a pip on the analog display. The grid had automatically adjusted to a 500-mile scale with the positions of the intruder and Aztec separated by almost the width of the instrument face. The Aztec seemed to have a clear edge in the race for the moon. Prochaska became aware of the newcomer but refrained from questions, nor did Crag volunteer any information.

FIRST ON THE MOON

Just now he wasn't worrying about the East World rocket. Not at this point. With Drone Able riding to starboard, the Aztec was moving at an ever slower rate of speed. It would continue to decelerate, slowed by the earth's pull as it moved outward, traveling on inertial force since the silencing of its engines. By the time it reached the neutral zone where the moon and earth gravispheres canceled each other, the Aztec would have just enough speed left to coast into the moon's field of influence. Then it would accelerate again, picking up speed until slowed by its braking rockets. That was the hour that occupied his thoughts—a time when he would be called upon for split-second decisions coming in waves.

He tried to anticipate every contingency. The mass ratio necessary to inject the Aztec into its moon trajectory had precluded fuel beyond the absolute minimum needed. The rocket would approach the moon in an elliptical path, correct its heading to a north-south line relative to the planet and decelerate in a tight spiral. At a precise point in space he would have to start using the braking rockets, slow the ship until they occupied an exact point in the infinite space-time continuum, then let down into cliff-brimmed Arzachel, a bleak, airless, utterly alien wasteland with but one virtue: Uranium. That and the fact that it represented the gateway to the Solar System.

He mentally reviewed the scene a hundred times. He would do this and this and that. He rehearsed each step, each operation, each fleeting second in which all the long years of planning would summate in victory or disaster. He was the X in the equation in which the Y-scale was represented by the radar altimeter. He would juggle speed, deceleration, altitude, mass and a dozen other variables, keeping them in delicate balance. Nor could he forget for one second the hostile architecture of their destination.

For all practical purposes Arzachel was a huge hole sunk

in the moon—a vast depression undoubtedly broken by rocks, rills, rough lava outcrops. The task struck him as similar to trying to land a high-speed jet in a well shaft. Well, almost as bad.

He tried to anticipate possible contingencies, formulating his responses to each. He was, he thought, like an actor preparing for his first night. Only this time there would be no repeat performance. The critics were the gods of chance in a strictly one-night stand.

Gotch was the man who had placed him here. But the responsibility was all his. Gotch! All he gave a damn about was the moon—a chunk of real estate scorned by its Maker. Crag bit his lip ruefully. Stop feeling sorry for yourself, boy, he thought. You asked for it—practically begged for it. Now you've got it.

By the end of the second day the novelty of space had worn off. Crag and Prochaska routinely checked the myriad of instruments jammed into the faces of the consoles: Meteorite impact counters, erosion counters, radiation counters—counters of all kinds. Little numbers on dials and gauges that told man how he was faring in the wastelands of the universe. Nagel kept a special watch on the oxygen pressure gauge. Meteorite damage had been one of Gotch's fears. A hole the size of a pinhead could mean eventual death through oxygen loss, hence Nagel seldom let a half-hour pass without checking the readings.

Crag and Prochaska spelled each other in brief catnaps. Larkwell, with no duties to perform, was restless. At first he had passed long hours at the viewports, uttering exclamations of surprise and delight from time to time. But sight of the ebony sky with its fields of strewn jewels had, in the end, tended to make him moody. He spent most of the second day dozing.

Nagel kept busy prowling through the oxygen gear, testing

connections and making minor adjustments. His seeming concern with the equipment bothered Crag. The narrow escape with the time bomb had robbed him of his confidence in the crew. He told himself the bomb could have been planted during the last security shakedown. But a "sleeper" in security seemed highly unlikely. So did a "sleeper" in the Aztec. Everyone of them, he knew, had been scanned under the finest security microscope almost from birth to the moment each had climbed the tall ladder leading to the space cabin.

He covertly watched Nagel, wondering if his prowling was a form of escape, an effort to forget his fears. He was beginning to understand the stark reality of Nagel's terror. It had been mirrored in his face, a naked, horrible dread, during the recent emergency. No . . . he wasn't the saboteur type. Larkwell, maybe. Perhaps Prochaska. But not Nagel. A saboteur would have iron nerves, a cold, icy fanaticism that never considered danger. But supposing the man were a consummate actor, his fear a mask to conceal his purpose?

He debated the pros and cons. In the end he decided it would not be politic to forbid Nagel to handle the gear during flight. He was, after all, their oxygen equipment specialist. He contented himself with keeping a sharp watch on Nagel's activities—a situation Nagel seemed unmindful of. He seemed to have lost some of his earlier fear. His face was alert, almost cheerful at times; yet it held the attitude of watchful waiting.

Despite his liking for Prochaska, Crag couldn't forget that he had failed to find the time bomb in a panel he had twice searched. Still, the console's complex maze of wiring and tubes had made an excellent hiding place. He had to admit he was lucky to have found it himself. He tried to push his suspicions from his mind without relaxing his vigilance. It was a hard job.

By the third day the enemy missile had become a prime factor in the things he found to worry about. The intruder rocket had drawn closer. Alpine warned that the race was neck and neck. It had either escaped earth at a higher speed or had continued to accelerate beyond the escape point. Crag regarded the reason as purely academic. The hard fact was that it would eventually overtake the still decelerating Aztec. Just now it was a pip on the analog, a pip which before long would loom as large as Drone Able, perhaps as close. He tried to assess its meaning, vexed that Alpine seemed to be doing so little to help in the matter.

Later Larkwell spotted the pip made by the East's rocket on the scope. That let the cat out of the bag as far as Crag was concerned. Soberly he informed them of its origin. Larkwell bit his lip thoughtfully. Nagel furrowed his brow, seemingly lost in contemplation. Prochaska's expression never changed. Crag assessed each reaction. In fairness, he also assessed his own feeling toward each of the men. He felt a positive dislike of Nagel and a positive liking for Prochaska. Larkwell was a neutral. He seemed to be a congenial, open-faced man who wore his feelings in plain sight. But there was a quality about him which, try as he would, he could not put his finger on.

Nagel, he told himself, must have plenty on the ball. After all, he had passed through a tough selection board. Just because the man's personality conflicted with his own was no grounds for suspicion. But the same reasoning could apply to the others. The fact remained—at least Gotch seemed certain—that his crew numbered a ringer among them. He was mulling it over when the communicator came to life. The message was in moon code.

It came slowly, widely spaced, as if Gotch realized Crag's limitations in handling the intricate cipher system evolved especially for this one operation. Learning it had caused him many a sleepless night. He copied the message letter by letter, his understanding blanked by the effort to decipher it. He finished, then quickly read the two scant lines:

"Blank channel to Alp unless survival need."

He studied the message for a long moment. Gotch was telling him not to contact Alpine Base unless it were a life or death matter. Not that everything connected with the operation wasn't a life or death matter, he thought grimly. He decided the message was connected with the presence of the rocket now riding astern and to one side of the Aztec and her drone. He guessed the Moon Code had been used to prevent possible pickup by the intruder rather than any secrecy involving his own crew.

He quietly passed the information to Prochaska. The Chief listened, nodding, his eyes going to the analog.

According to his computations, the enemy rocket—Prochaska had dubbed it Bandit—would pass abeam of Drone Able slightly after they entered the moon's gravitational field, about 24,000 miles above the planet's surface. Then what? He pursed his lips vexedly. Bandit was a factor that had to be considered, but just how he didn't know. One thing was certain. The East knew about the load of uranium in Crater Arzachel. That, then, was the destination of the other rocket. Among the many X unknowns he had to solve, a new X had been added; the rocket from behind the Iron Curtain. Something told him this would be the biggest X of all.

CHAPTER 7

IF COLONEL Michael Gotch were worried, he didn't show it. He puffed complacently on his black briar pipe watching and listening to the leathery-faced man across from him. His visitor was angular, about sixty, with gray-black hair and hard-squinted eyes. A livid scar bit deep into his forehead; his mouth was a cold thin slash in his face. He wore the uniform of a Major General in the United States Air Force. The uniform did not denote the fact that its wearer was M.I.—Military Intelligence. His name was Leonard Telford.

"So that's the way it looks," General Telford was saying. "The enemy is out to get Arzachel at all costs. Failing that, they'll act to keep us from it."

"They wouldn't risk war," Gotch stated calmly.

"No, but neither would we. That's the damnable part of it," the General agreed. "The next war spells total annihilation. But for that very reason they can engage in sabotage and hostile acts with security of knowledge that we won't go to war. Look at them now—the missile attack on the Aztec, the time bomb plant, the way they operate their networks right in our midst. Pure audacity. Hell, they've even got an agent *en route* to the moon. On our rocket at that."

The Colonel nodded uncomfortably. The presence of a saboteur on the Aztec represented a bungle in his department. The General was telling him so in a not too gentle way.

"I seem to recall I was in Astrakhan myself a few years back," he reminded.

"Oh, sure, we build pretty fair networks ourselves," the General said blandly. He looked at Gotch and a rare smile crossed his face. "How did you like the dancing girls in Gorik's, over by the shore?"

Gotch looked startled, then grinned. "Didn't know you'd ever been that far in, General."

"Uh-huh, same time you were."

"Well, I'll be damned," Gotch breathed softly. There was a note of respect in his voice. The General was silent for a moment.

"But the Caspian's hot now."

"Meaning?"

"Warheads—with the name Arzachel writ large across the nose cones." He eyed Gotch obliquely. "If we secure Arzachel first, they'll blow it off the face of the moon." They looked at each other silently. Outside a jet engine roared to life.

The moon filled the sky. It was gigantic, breath-taking, a monstrous sphere of cratered rock moving in the eternal silence of space with ghostly radiance, heedless that a minute mote bearing alien life had entered its gravitational field. It moved in majesty along its orbit some 2,300 miles every hour, alternately approaching to within 222,000 miles of its Earth Mother, retreating to over 252,000 miles measuring its strides by some strange cosmic clock.

The Apennines, a rugged mountain range jutting 20,000 feet above the planet's surface, was clearly visible. It rose near the Crater Eratosthenes, running northwest some 200 miles to form the southwest boundary of Mare Imbrium. The towering Leibnitz and Dorfel Mountains were visible near the edge of the disc. South along the terminator, the border between night and day, lay Ptolemaeus, Alphons, and Arzachel.

Crag and Prochaska studied its surface, picking out the flat areas which early astronomers had mistaken for seas and which still bore the names of seas. The giant enclosure Clavius, the lagoon-like Plato and ash-strewn Copernicus held their attention. Crag studied the north-south line along which Arzachel lay, wondering again if they could seek out such a relatively small area in the jumbled, broken, twisted land beneath them.

At some 210,000 miles from earth the Aztec had decelerated to a little over 300 miles per hour. Shortly after entering the moon's gravisphere it began to accelerate again. Crag studied the enemy rocket riding astern. It would be almost abreast them in short time, off to one side of the silver drone. It, too, was accelerating.

"Going to be nip and tuck," he told Prochaska. The Chief nodded.

"Don't like the looks of that stinker," he grunted.

Crag watched the analog a moment longer before turning to the quartz viewport. His eyes filled with wonder. For untold ages lovers had sung of the moon, philosophers had pondered its mysteries, astronomers had scanned and mapped every visible mile of its surface until selenography had achieved an exactness comparable to earth cartography. Scientists had proved beyond doubt that the moon wasn't made of green cheese. But no human eye had ever beheld its surface as Crag was doing now—Crag, Prochaska, Larkwell and Nagel. The latter two were peering through the side ports. Prochaska and Crag shared the forward panel. It was a tribute to the event that no word was spoken. Aside from the Chief's occasional checks on Drone Able and Bandit —the name stuck—the four pairs of eyes seldom left the satellite's surface.

The landing plan called for circling the moon during which they were to maneuver Drone Able into independent orbit. It was Crag's job to bring the Aztec down at a precise point in Crater Arzachel and the Chief's job to handle the drone landings, a task as ticklish as landing the Aztec itself.

The spot chosen for landing was in an area where the Crater's floor was broken by a series of rills—wide, shallow cracks the earth scientists hoped would give protection against the fall of meteorites. Due to lack of atmosphere the particles in space, ranging from dust grains to huge chunks of rock, were more lethal than bullets. They were another unknown in the gamble for the moon. A direct hit by even a grain-sized particle could puncture a space suit and bring instant death. A large one could utterly destroy the rocket itself. Larkwell's job was to construct an airlock in one of the rills from durable lightweight prefabricated plastiblocks carried in the drones. Such an airlock would protect them from all but vertically falling meteorites.

Crag felt almost humble in the face of the task they were undertaking. He knew his mind alone could grasp but a minute part of the knowledge that went into making the expedition possible. Their saving lay in the fact they were but agents, protoplasmic extensions of a complex of computers, scientists, plans which had taken years to formulate, and a man named Michael Gotch who had said:

"You will land on Arzachel."

He initiated the zero phase by ordering the crew into their pressure suits. Prochaska took over while he donned his own bulky garment, grimacing as he pulled the heavy helmet over his shoulders. Later, in the last moments of descent, he would snap down the face plate and pressurize the suit. Until then he wanted all the freedom the bulky garments would allow.

"Might as well get used to it." Prochaska grinned. He flexed his arms experimentally.

Larkwell grunted. "Wait till they're pressurized. You'll think rigor mortis has set in."

Crag grinned. "That's a condition I'm opposed to."

"Amen." Larkwell gave a weak experimental jump and promptly smacked his head against the low overhead. He was smiling foolishly when Nagel snapped at him:

"One more of those and you'll be walking around the moon without a pressure suit." He peevishly insisted on examining the top of the helmet for damage.

Crag fervently hoped they wouldn't need the suits for landing. Any damage that would allow the Aztec's oxygen to escape would in itself be a death sentence, even though death might be dragged over the long period of time it would take to die for lack of food. An intact space cabin represented the only haven in which they could escape from the cumbersome garments long enough to tend their biological needs.

Imperceptibly the sensation of weight returned, but it was not the body weight of earth. Even on the moon's surface they would weigh but one-sixth their normal weight.

"Skipper, look." Prochaska's startled exclamation drew Crag's eyes to the radarscope. Bandit had made minute corrections in its course.

"They're using steering rockets," Crag mused, trying to assess its meaning.

"Doesn't make sense," said Prochaska. "They can't have that kind of power to spare. They'll need every bit they have for landing."

"What's up?" Larkwell peered over their shoulders, eyeing the radarscope. Crag bit off an angry retort. Larkwell sensed the rebuff and returned away. They kept their eyes glued to the scope. Bandit maneuvered to a position slightly behind and to one side of the silver drone. Crag looked out the side port. Bandit was clearly visible, a monstrous cylinder boring through the void with cold precision. There was something ominous about it. He felt the hair prickle at the nape of his neck. Larkwell moved alongside him.

Bandit made another minute correction. White vapor shot from its tail and it began to move ahead.

"Using rocket power," Crag grunted. "Damn if I can figure that one out."

"Looks crazy to me. I should think—" Prochaska's voice froze. A minute pip broke off from Bandit, boring through space toward the silver drone.

"Warhead!" Crag roared the word with cold anger.

Prochaska cursed softly.

One second Drone Able was there, riding serenely through space. The next it disintegrated, blasted apart by internal explosions. Seconds later only fragments of the drone were visible.

Prochaska stared at Crag, his face bleak. Crag's brain

reeled. He mentally examined what had happened, culling his thoughts until one cold fact remained.

"Mistaken identity," he said softly. "They thought it was the Aztec."

"Now what?"

"Now we hope they haven't any more warheads." Crag mulled the possibility. "Considering weight factors, I'd guess they haven't. Besides, there's no profit in wasting a warhead on a drone."

"We hope." Prochaska studied Bandit through the port, and licked his lips nervously. "Think we ought to contact Alpine?"

Crag weighed the question. Despite the tight beam, any communication could be a dead giveaway. On the other hand, Bandit either had the capacity to destroy them or it didn't. If it did, well, there wasn't much they could do about it. He reached a decision and nodded to Prochaska, then began coding his thoughts.

He had trouble getting through on the communicator. Finally he got a weak return signal, then sent a brief report. Alpine acknowledged and cut off the air.

"What now?" Prochaska asked, when Crag had finished.

He shrugged and turned to the side port without answering. Bandit loomed large, a long thick rocket with an oddly blunted nose. A monster that was as deadly as it looked.

"Big," he surmised. "Much bigger than this chunk of hardware."

"Yeah, a regular battleship," Prochaska assented. He grinned crookedly. "In more ways than one."

Crag sensed movement at his shoulder and turned his head. Nagel was studying the radarscope over his shoulder. Surprise lit his narrow face.

"The drone?"

"Destroyed," Crag said bruskly. "Bandit had a warhead."

Nagel looked startled, then retreated to his seat without a word. Crag returned his attention to the enemy rocket.

"What do you think?" he asked Prochaska.

His answer was solemn. "It spells trouble."

CHAPTER 8

AT A PRECISE point in space spelled out by the Alpine computers Crag applied the first braking rockets. He realized that the act had been an immediate tip-off to the occupants of the other rocket. No matter, he thought. Sooner or later they had to discover it was the drone they had destroyed Slowly, almost imperceptibly, their headlong flight was slowed. He nursed the rockets with care. There was no fuel to spare, no energy to waste, no room for error. Everything had been worked out long beforehand; he was merely the agent of execution.

The sensation of weight gradually increased. He ordered Larkwell and Nagel into their seats in strapdown position. He and Prochaska shortly followed, but he left his shoulder harnessing loose to give his arms the vital freedom he needed for the intricate maneuvers ahead.

The moon rushed toward them at an appalling rate. Its surface was a harsh grille work of black and white, a nightmarish scape of pocks and twisted mountains of rock rimming the flat lunar plains. It was, he thought, the geometry of a maniac. There was no softness, no blend of light and shadow, only terrible cleavages between black and white. Yet there was a beauty that gripped his imagination;

the raw, stark beauty of a nature undefiled by life. No eye had ever seen the canopy of the heavens from the bleak surface below; no flower had ever wafted in a lunar breeze.

Prochaska nudged his arm and indicated the scope. Bandit was almost abreast them. Crag nodded understandingly.

"No more warheads."

"Guess we're just loaded with luck," Prochaska agreed wryly.

They watched . . . waited . . . mindless of time. Crag felt the tension building inside him. Occasionally he glanced at the chronometer, itching for action. The wait seemed interminable. Minutes or hours? He lost track of time.

All at once his hands and mind were busy with the braking rockets, dials, meters. First the moon had been a pallid giant in the sky; next it filled the horizon. The effect was startling. The limb of the moon, seen as a shallow curved horizon, no longer was smooth. It appeared as a rugged sawtoothed arc, somehow reminding him of the Devil's Golf Course in California's Death Valley. It was weird and wonderful, and slightly terrifying.

Prochaska manned the automatic camera to record the orbital and landing phases. He spotted the Crater of Ptolemaeus first, near the center-line of the disc. Crag made a minute correction with the steering rockets. The enemy rocket followed suit. Prochaska gave a short harsh laugh without humor.

"Looks like we're piloting them in. Jeepers, you'd think they could do their own navigation."

"Shows the confidence they have in us," Crag retorted.

They flashed high above Ptolemaeus, a crater ninety miles in diameter rimmed by walls three thousand feet high. The crater fled by below them. South lay Alphons; and farther south, Arzachel, with walls ten thousand feet high rimming its vast depressed interior.

Prochaska observed quietly: "Nice rugged spot. It's going to take some doing."

"Amen."

"I'm beginning to get that what-the-hell-am-I-doing-here feeling."

"I've had it right along," Crag confided.

They caught only a fleeting look at Arzachel before it rushed into the background. Crag touched the braking rockets from time to time, gently, precisely, keeping his eyes moving between the radar altimeter and speed indicator while the Chief fed him the course data.

The back side of the moon was spinning into view—the side of the moon never before seen by human eyes. Prochaska whistled softly. A huge mountain range interlaced with valleys and chasms pushed some thirty thousand feet into the lunar skies. Long streaks of ochre and brown marked its sides, the first color they had seen on the moon. Flat highland plains crested between the peaks were dotted with strange monolithic structures almost geometrical in their distribution.

Prochaska was shooting the scene with the automatic camera. Crag twisted around several times to nod reassuringly to Nagel and Larkwell but each time they were occupied with the side ports, oblivious of his gesture. To his surprise Nagel's face was rapt, almost dreamy, completely absorbed by the stark lands below. Larkwell, too, was quiet with wonder.

The jagged mountains fell away to a great sea, larger even than Mare Imbrium, and like Mare Imbrium, devoid of life. A huge crater rose from its center, towering over twenty thousand feet. Beyond lay more mountains. The land between was a wild tangle of rock, a place of unutterable desolation. Crag was fascinated and depressed at the same time. The Aztec was closing around the moon in a tight spiral.

FIRST ON THE MOON

The alien landscape drew visibly nearer. He switched his attention between the braking rockets and instruments, trying to manage a quick glance at the scope. Prochaska caught his look.

"Bandit's up on us," he confirmed.

Crag uttered a vile epithet and Prochaska grinned. He liked to hear him growl, taking it as a good sign.

Crag glanced worriedly at the radar altimeter and hit the braking rockets harder. The quick deceleration gave the impression of added weight, pushing them hard against their chest harnesses.

He found it difficult to make the precise hand movements required. The Aztec was dropping with frightening rapidity. They crossed more mountains, seas, craters, great chasms. Time had become meaningless—had ceased to exist. The sheer bleakness of the face of the moon gripped his imagination. He saw it as the supreme challenge, the magnitude of which took his breath. He was Cortez scanning the land of the Aztecs. More, for this stark lonely terrain had never felt the stir of life. No benevolent Maker had created this chaos. It was an inferno without fire—a hell of a kind never known on earth. It was the handiwork of a nature on a rampage—a maddened nature whose molding clay had been molten lava.

He stirred the controls, moved them further, holding hard. The braking rockets shook the ship, coming through the bulkheads as a faint roar. The ground came up fast. Still the landscape fled by—fled past for seeming days.

Prochaska announced wonderingly. "We've cleared the back side. You're on the landing run, Skipper."

Crag nodded grimly, thinking it was going to be rough. Each second, each split second had to be considered. There was no margin for error. No second chance. He checked and re-checked his instruments, juggling speed against altitude.

Ninety-mile wide Ptolemaeus was coming around again—

fast. He caught a glimpse through the floor port. It was a huge saucer, level at the bottom, rimmed by low cliffs which looked as though they had been carved from obsidian. The floor was split by irregular chasms, punctuated by sharp high pinnacles. It receded and Alphons rushed to meet them. The Aztec was dropping fast. Too fast? Crag looked worriedly at the radar altimeter and hit the braking rockets harder. Alphons passed more slowly. They fled south, a slim needle in the lunar skies.

"Arzachel . . ." He breathed the name almost reverently.

Prochaska glanced out the side port before hurriedly consulting the instruments. Thirty thousand feet! He glanced worriedly at Crag. The ground passed below them at a fantastic speed. They seemed to be dropping faster. The stark face of the planet hurtled to meet them.

"Fifteen thousand feet," Prochaska half-whispered. Crag nodded. "Twelve thousand . . . ten . . . eight . . ." The Chief continued to chant the altitude readings in a strained voice. Up until then the face of the moon had seemed to rush toward the Aztec. All at once it changed. Now it was the Aztec that rushed across the hostile land—rushing and dropping. "Three thousand . . . two thousand . . ." They flashed high above a great cliff which fell away for some ten thousand feet. At its base began the plain of Arzachel.

Out of the corner of his eye Crag saw that Bandit was leading them. But higher . . . much higher. Now it was needling into the purple-black—straight up. He gave a quick, automatic instrument check. The braking rockets were blasting hard. He switched one hand to the steering rockets.

Zero minute was coming up. Bandit was ahead, but higher. It could, he thought, be a photo finish. Suddenly he remembered his face plate and snapped it shut, opening the oxygen valve. The suit grew rigid on his body and hampered his arms. He cursed softly and looked sideways at Prochaska. He was having the same difficulty. Crag managed a quick over-the-shoulder glance at Larkwell and Nagel. Everything seemed okay.

He took a deep breath and applied full deceleration with the braking jets and simultaneously began manipulating the steering rockets. The ship vibrated from stem to stern. The forward port moved upward; the face of the moon swished past and disappeared. Bandit was lost to sight. The ship trembled, shuddered and gave a violent wrench. Crag was thrown forward.

The Aztec began letting down, tail first. It was a sickening moment. The braking rockets astern, heavy with smoke, thundered through the hull. The smoke blanketed out the ports. The cabin vibrated. He straightened the nose with the steering rockets, letting the ship fall in a vertical attitude, tail first. He snapped a glance at the radar altimeter and punched a button.

A servo mechanism somewhere in the ship started a small motor. A tubular spidery metal framework was projected out from the tail, extending some twenty feet before it locked into position. It was a failing device intended to absorb the energy generated by the landing impact.

Prochaska looked worriedly out the side port. Crag followed his eyes. Small details on the plain of Arzachel loomed large—pits, cracks, low ridges of rock. Suddenly the plain was an appalling reality. Rocky fingers reached to grip them. He twisted his head until he caught sight of Bandit. It was moving down, tail first, but it was still high in the sky. Too high, he thought. He took a fast look at the radar altimeter and punched the full battery of braking rockets again. The force on his body seemed unbearable. Blood was forced into his head, blurring his vision. His ears buzzed and his spine seemed to be supporting some gigantic weight. The pressure eased and the ground began moving up more slowly. The rockets were blasting steadily.

For a split-second the ship seemed to hang in mid-air followed by a violent shock. The cabin teetered, then smashed onto the plain, swaying as the framework projecting from the tail crumpled. The shock drove them hard into their seats. They sat for a moment before full realization dawned. They were down—alive!

Crag and Prochaska simultaneously began shucking their safety belts. Crag was first. He sprang to the side port just in time to see the last seconds of Bandit's landing. It came down fast, a perpendicular needle stabbing toward the lunar surface. Flame spewed from its braking rockets; white smoke enveloped its nose.

Fast . . . too fast, he thought. Suddenly the flame licked out. Fuel error. The thought flashed through his mind. The fuel Bandit had wasted in space maneuvering to destroy the drone had left it short. The rocket seemed to hang in the sky for a scant second before it plummeted straight down, smashing into the stark lunar landscape. The Chief had reached his side just in time to witness the crash.

"That's all for them," he said. "Can't say I'm sorry."

"Serves 'em damn well right," growled Crag. He became conscious of Nagel and Larkwell crowding to get a look and obligingly moved to one side without taking his eyes from the scene. He tried to judge Bandit's distance.

"Little over two miles," he estimated aloud.

"You can't tell in this vacuum," Prochaska advised. "Your eyes play you tricks. Wait'll I try the scope." A moment later he turned admiringly from the instrument.

"Closer to three miles. Pretty good for a green hand."

Crag laughed, a quiet laugh of self-satisfaction, and said, "I could use a little elbow room. Any volunteers?"

"Liberty call," Prochaska sang out. "All ashore who's going ashore. The gals are waiting."

"I'm a little tired of this sardine can, myself," Larkwell put in. "Let's get on our Sunday duds and blow. I'd like to do the town." There was a murmur of assent. Nagel, who

FIRST ON THE MOON 71

was monitoring the oxygen pressure gauge, spoke affirmatively. "No leaks."

"Good," Crag said with relief. He took a moment off to feel exultant but the mood quickly vanished. There was work ahead—sheer drudgery.

"Check suit pressure," he ordered.

They waited a moment longer while they tested pressure, the interphones, and adjusted to the lack of body weight before Crag moved toward the hatch. Prochaska prompted them to actuate their temperature controls:

"It's going to be hot out there."

Crag nodded, checked his temperature dial and started to open the hatch. The lock-lever resisted his efforts for a moment. He tested the dogs securing the door. Several of them appeared jammed. Panic touched his mind. He braced his body, moving against one of the lock levers with all his strength. It gave, then another. He loosened the last lock braced against the blast of escaping air. The hatch exploded open.

He stood for a moment looking at the ground, some twenty feet below. The metal framework now crumpled below the tail had done its work. It had struck, failing, and in doing so had absorbed a large amount of impact energy which otherwise would have been absorbed by the body of the rocket with possible damage to the space cabin.

The Aztec's tail fins were buried in what appeared to be a powdery ash. The rocket was canted slightly but, he thought, not dangerously so. Larkwell broke out the rope ladder provided for descent and was looking busy. Now it was his turn to shine. He hooked the ladder over two pegs and let the other end fall to the ground. He tested it then straightened up and turned to Crag.

"You may depart, Sire."

Crag grinned and started down the ladder. It was clumsy work. The bulk and rigidity of his suit made his movements uncertain, difficult. He descended slowly, testing each step. He hesitated at the last rung, thinking: *This is it!* He let his foot dangle above the surface for a moment before plunging it down into the soft ash mantle, then walked a few feet, ankle deep in a fine gray powder. First human foot to touch the moon, he thought. The first human foot ever to step beyond the world. Yeah, the human race was on the way—led by Adam Philip Crag. He felt good.

It occurred to him then that he was not the real victor. That honor belonged to a man 240,000 miles away. Gotch had won the moon. It had been the opaque-eyed Colonel who had directed the conquest. He, Crag, was merely a foot soldier. Just one of the troops. All at once he felt humble.

Prochaska came down next, followed by Nagel. Larkwell was last. They stood in a half-circle looking at each other, awed by the thing they had done. No one spoke. They shifted their eyes outward, hungrily over the plain, marveling at the world they had inherited. It was a bleak, hostile world encompassed in a bowl whose vast depressed interior alternately was burned and frozen by turn. To their north the rim of Arzachel towered ten thousand feet, falling away as it curved over the horizon to the east and west. The plain to the south was a flat expanse of gray punctuated by occasional rocky knolls and weird, needle-sharp pinnacles, some of which towered to awesome heights.

Southeast a long narrow spur of rock rose and crawled over the floor of the crater for several miles before it dipped again into its ashy bed. Crag calculated that a beeline to Bandit would just about skirt the southeast end of the spur. Another rock formation dominated the middle-expanse of the plain to the south. It rose, curving over the crater floor like the spinal column of some gigantic lizard—a great crescent with its horns pointed toward their present position. Prochaska promptly dubbed it "Backbone Ridge," a name that stuck.

FIRST ON THE MOON 73

Crag suddenly remembered what he had to do, and coughed meaningfully into his lip mike. The group fell silent. He faced the distant northern cliffs and began to speak:

"I, Adam Crag, by the authority vested in me by the Government of the United States of America, do hereby claim this land, and all the lands of the moon, as legal territory of the United States of America, to be a dominion of the United States of America, subject to its Government and laws."

When he finished, he was quiet for a minute. "For the record, this is Pickering Field. I think he'd like that," he added. There was a lump in his throat.

Prochaska said quietly, "Gotch will like it, too. Hadn't we better record that and transmit it to Alpine?"

"It's already recorded." Crag grinned. "All but the Pickering Field part. Gotch wrote it out himself."

"Confident bastard." Larkwell smiled. "He had a lot more faith than I did."

"Especially the way you brought that stovepipe down," Nagel interjected. There was a moment of startled silence.

Prochaska said coldly. "I hope you do your job as well."

Nagel looked provocatively at him but didn't reply.

Larkwell had been studying the terrain. "Wish Able had made it," he said wistfully. "I'd like to get started on that airlock. It's going to be a honey to build."

"Amen." Crag swept his eyes over the ashy surface. "The scientists figure that falling meteorites may be our biggest hazard."

"Not if we follow the plan of building our airlock in a rill," Larkwell interjected. "Then the only danger would be from stuff coming straight down."

"Agreed. But the fact remains that we lost Able. We'll have to chance living in the Aztec until Drone Baker arrives."

"If it makes it."

"It'll make it," Crag answered with certainty. Their safe landing had boosted his confidence. They'd land Baker and Charlie, in that order, he thought. They'd locate a shallow rill; then they'd build an airlock to protect them against chance meteorites. That's the way they'd do it; one . . . two . . . three. . . .

"We've got it whipped," Prochaska observed, but his voice didn't hold the certainty of his words.

Crag said, "I was wondering if we couldn't assess the danger. It might not be so great . . ."

"How?" Prochaska asked curiously.

"No wind, no air, no external forces to disturb the ash mantle, except for meteorites. Any strike would leave a trace. We might smooth off a given area and check for hits after a couple of days. That would give some idea of the danger." He faced Prochaska.

"What do you think?"

"But the ash itself is meteorite dust," he protested.

"We could at least chart the big hits—those large enough to damage the rocket."

"We'll know if any hit," Larkwell prophesied grimly.

"Maybe not," Nagel cut in ."Supposing it's pinhole size? The air could seep out and we wouldn't know it until too late."

Crag said decisively. "That means we'll have to maintain a watch over the pressure gauge."

"That won't help if it's a big chunk." Prochaska scraped his toe through the ash. "The possibility's sort of disconcerting."

"Too damned many occupational hazards for me," Larkwell ventured. "I must have had rocks in my head when I volunteered for this one."

"All brawn and no brain." Crag gave a wry smile. "That's the kind of fodder that's needed for deep space."

Prochaska said, "We ought to let Gotch know he's just acquired a few more acres."

"Right." Crag hesitated a moment. "Then we'll check out on Bandit."

"Why?" Larkwell asked.

"There might be some survivors."

"Let them rot," Nagel growled.

"That's for me to decide," Crag said coldly. He stared hard at the oxygen man. "We're still human."

Nagel snapped, "They're damned murderers."

"That's no reason we should be." Crag turned back toward the ladder. When he reached it, he paused and looked skyward. The sun was a precise circle of intolerable white light set amid the ebony of space. The stars seemed very close.

The space cabin was a vacuum. At Nagel's suggestion they kept pressure to a minimum to preserve oxygen. When they were out of their suits, Prochaska got on the radio. He had difficulty raising Alpine Base, working for several minutes before he got an answering signal. When the connection was made, Crag moved into Prochaska's place and switched to his ear insert microphone. He listened to the faint slightly metallic voice for a moment before he identified it as Gotch's. He thought: *The Old Man must be living in the radio shack.* He adjusted his headset and sent a lengthy report.

If Gotch were jubilant over the fruition of his dream, he carefully concealed it. He congratulated Crag and the crew, speaking in precise formal terms, and almost immediately launched into a barrage of questions regarding their next step. The Colonel's reaction nettled him. Lord, he should be jubilant . . . jumping with joy . . . waltzing the telephone gal. Instead he was speaking with a business-as-usual manner. Gotch left it up to Crag on whether or not to attempt a rescue expedition.

"But not if it endangers the expedition in any way," he added. He informed him that Drone Baker had been launched without mishap. "Just be ready for her," he cautioned. "And again—congratulations, Commander." There was a pause..

"I think Pickering Field is a fitting name." The voice in the earphones died away and Crag found himself listening to the static of space. He pulled the sets off and turned to Nagel.

"How much oxygen would a man need for a round trip to Bandit, assuming a total distance of seven miles."

"It's not that far," Prochaska reminded.

"There might be detours."

Nagel calculated rapidly. "An extra cylinder would do it."

"Okay, Larkwell and I'll go. You and Prochaska stand by." Crag caught the surprised look on the Chief's face.

"There might be communication problems," he explained. Privately, he had decided that no man would be left alone until the mystery of the time bomb was cleared up.

Prochaska nodded. The arrangement made sense. Nagel appeared pleased that he didn't have to make the long trek. Larkwell, on the other hand, seemed glad to have been chosen.

CHAPTER 9

THERE IS NO DAWN on the moon, no dusk, no atmosphere to catch and spread the light of the sun. When the lunar night ends—a night two earth weeks long—the sun simply pops over the horizon, bringing its intolerable heat. But the sky remains black—black and sprinkled with stars agleam with a light unknown on earth. At night the temperature is 250 degrees below zero; by day it is the heat of boiling water. Yet the sun is but an intense circle of white aloft in a nigrescent sky. It was a world such as Crag had scarcely dreamed of—alien, hostile, fantastic in its architecture—a bizarre world spawned by a nature in revolt.

Crag stopped to adjust the temperature control on his suit. He started to mop his brow before he remembered the helmet. Larkwell saw the gesture, and behind his thick face plate his lips wrinkled in a grin. "Go on, scratch it," he challenged.

"This moon's going to take a lot of getting used to." Crag swept his eyes over the bleak plain. "And they send four men to conquer this."

"It ain't conquered yet," Larkwell spat.

Crag's answer was a sober reflection. "No, it isn't," he said quietly. He contemplated the soot-filled sky, its magic lanterns, then looked down again at the plain.

"Let's get moving."

It was dawn—dawn in the sense that the sun had climbed above the horizon. The landing had been planned for sunup —the line which divided night from day—to give them the benefit of a two-week day before another instantaneous onslaught of night.

They moved slowly across the ashy floor of the crater, occasionally circling small knolls or jagged rock outcroppings. Despite the cumbersome suits and the burden of the extra oxygen cylinder each carried, they made good time. Crag led the way with Larkwell close behind, threading his way toward the spot where the enemy rocket had fallen from the sky. They had to stop several times to rest and regulate their temperature controls. Despite the protective garments they were soon sweating and panting, gasping for breath with the feeling of suffocation. Crag felt the water trickling down his body in rivulets and began to itch, a sensation that was almost a pain.

"It's not going to be a picnic," Larkwell complained. His voice sounded exhausted in the earphones.

Crag grunted without answering. His feet ploughed up little spurts of dust which fell as quickly as they rose. Like water dropping, he thought. He wondered how long they would be able to endure the heat. Could they possibly adapt their bodies to such an environment? What of the cold of night? The questions bothered him. He tried to visualize what it would be like to plunge from boiling day to the bitterly cold night within the space of moments. Would they be able to take it? He grinned to himself. They'd find out!

At the next halt they looked back at the Aztec.

"We don't seem to be getting anywhere," Larkwell observed. Crag contemplated the rocket. He was right. The ship seemed almost as large and clear as ever.

"Your eyes trick you," he said. "It's just another thing we'll have to get used to." He let his eyes linger on the plain. It was washed with a brilliant light which even their glare shields didn't diminish. Each rock, each outcrop cast long black shadows—black silhouettes against the white ash. There were no grays, no intermediate shades. Everything was either black or white. His eyes began to ache and he turned them from the scene. He nodded at Larkwell and resumed his trek. He was trudging head down when he suddenly stopped. A chasm yawned at his feet.

"Mighty wide," Larkwell observed, coming up.

"Yeah," said Crag, indecisively. The rift was about twenty feet wide, its bottom lost in black shadows.

Larkwell studied the chasm carefully. "Might be just the rill we need for an airlock. If it's not too deep," he added. He picked up a boulder and dropped it over the edge, waiting expectantly. Crag chuckled. The construction man had forgotten that sound couldn't be transmitted through a vacuum. Larkwell caught the laugh in his earphones and smiled weakly.

He said sheepishly, "Something else to learn."

"We've plenty to learn." Crag looked both ways. To the right the chasm seemed to narrow and, although he wasn't sure, end.

"Let's try it," he suggested. Larkwell nodded agreement. They trudged along the edge of the fissure, walking slowly to conserve their energy. The plain became more uneven. Small outcroppings of black glassy rock punctured the ash, becoming more numerous as they progressed. Occasional saw-toothed needles pierced the sky. Several times they stopped and looked back at the Aztec. It was a black cylinder, smaller yet seemingly close.

Crag's guess was right. The chasm narrowed abruptly and terminated at the base of a small knoll. Both rockets were now hidden by intervening rocks. He hesitated before striking out, keeping Backbone Ridge to his right. The ground became progressively more uneven. They trudged onward for over a mile before he caught sight of the Aztec again. He paused, with the feeling something was wrong. Larkwell put it into words.

"Lost."

"Not lost, but off course." Crag took a moment to get his bearings and then struck out again thinking their oxygen supply couldn't stand many of these mistakes.

"How you doing, Skipper?"

Crag gave a start before remembering that Prochaska and Nagel were cut into their intercom.

"Lousy," he told them. He gave a brief run-down.

"Just happened to think that I could help guide you. I'll work you with the scope," Prochaska said.

"Of course," Crag exclaimed, wondering why they hadn't thought of it before. One thing was certain: they'd have to start remembering a lot of things. Thereafter, they checked with Prochaska every few minutes.

The ground constantly changed as they progressed. One moment it was level, dusty with ash; the next it was broken by low rocky ridges and interlacing chasms. Minutes extended into seeming hours and they had to stop for rest from time to time. Crag was leading the way across a small ravine when Larkwell's voice brought him up short:

"Commander, we're forgetting something."

"What?"

"Radcounters. Mine's whispering a tune I didn't like."

"Not a thing to worry about," Crag assured him. "The raw ores aren't that potent." Nevertheless he unhooked his counter and studied it. Larkwell was right. They were on hot ground but the count was low.

"Won't bother us a bit," he affirmed cheerfully.

Larkwell's answer was a grunt. Crag checked the instrument several times thinking that before long—when they were settled—they would mark off the boundaries of the lode. Gotch would want that. The count rose slightly. Once he caught Larkwell nervously consulting his meter. Clearly the construction boss wasn't too happy over their position. Crag wanted to tell him he had been reading too many Sunday supplements but didn't.

Prochaska broke in, "You're getting close." His voice was a faint whisper over the phones. "Maybe you'd better make a cautious approach."

Crag remembered the fate of Drone Able and silently agreed. Thereafter he kept his eyes peeled. They climbed a small knoll and saw Bandit. He abruptly halted, waiting until Larkwell reached his side.

The rocket lay at the base of the slope, which fell away before them. It was careened at a crazy angle with its base crumpled. A wide cleft running half way to its nose was visible. Crag studied the rocket carefully.

"Might still be oxygen in the space cabin," he ventured finally. "The break in the hull might not reach that far."

"It does," Larkwell corrected. His eyes, trained in construction work, had noted small cracks in the metal extending up alongside the hatch.

"No survivors in there," he grunted.

Crag said thoughtfully: "Might be, if they had on their pressure suits. And they would have," he added.

He hesitated before striking across the clearing, then began moving down the slope. Larkwell followed slowly. As he neared the rocket Crag saw that it lacked any type of failing device to absorb the landing impact. That, at least, had been one secret kept, he thought. He was wondering how to get into the space cabin when Larkwell solved the problem. He drew a thin hemp line from a leg pocket and began uncoiling it. Crag smiled approval.

"Never without one in the construction business," he explained. He studied Bandit. "Maybe I can hook it over the top of that busted tail fin, then work my way up the break in the hull."

"Let me try," Crag offered. The climb looked hazardous.

"This is my province." Larkwell snorted. He ran his eye over the ship before casting the line. He looked surprised when it shot high above the intended target point.

"Keep forgetting the low gravity," he apologized. He tried again. On the third throw he hooked the line over the torn tailfin. He rubbed his hands against his suit then started upward, climbing clumsily, each movement exaggerated by the bulky suit. He progressed slowly, testing each step. Crag held his breath. Larkwell gripped the line with his body swung outward, his feet planted against the vertical metal, reminding Crag of a human fly. He stopped to rest just below the level of the space cabin.

"Thought a man was supposed to be able to jump thirty feet on the moon," he panted.

"You can if you peel those duds off," Crag replied cheerfully. He ran his eye over the break noting the splintered metal. "Be careful of your suit."

Larkwell didn't answer. He was busy again trying to pull his body upward, using the break in the hull to obtain finger grips. Only the moon's low gravity allowed him to perform what looked like an impossible task. He finally reached a point alongside the hatch and paused, breathing heavily. He rested a moment, then carefully inserted his hand into the break in the hull. After a moment he withdrew it, and fumbled in his leg pocket withdrawing a switchblade knife.

"Got to cut through the lining," he explained. He worked the knife around inside the break for several minutes, then closed the blade and reinserted his hand, feeling around until he located the lockbar.

He tugged. It didn't give. He braced his body and exerted all of his strength. This time it moved. He rested a moment then turned his attention to the remaining doglocks. In short time he had the hatch open. Carefully, then, he pulled his body across to the black rectangle and disappeared inside.

"See anything?" Crag shifted his feet restlessly.

"Dead men." Larkwell's voice sounded relieved over the phones. "Smashed face plates." There was a long moment of silence. Crag waited impatiently.

"Just a second," he finally reported. "Looks like a live one." There was another interval of silence while Crag stewed. Finally he appeared in the opening with a hemp ladder.

"Knew they had to have some way of getting out of this trap," he announced triumphantly. He knelt and secured one end to the hatch combing and let the other end drop to the ground.

Crag climbed to meet him. Larkwell extended a hand and helped him through the hatch. One glance at the interior of the cabin told him that any life left was little short of a miracle. The man in the pilot's seat lay with his faceplate smashed against the instrument panel. The top of his fiberglass helmet had shattered and the top of his head was a bloody mess. A second crewman was sprawled over the communication console with his face smashed into the radarscope. His suit had been ripped from shoulder to waist and one leg was twisted at a crazy angle. Crag turned his eyes away.

"Here," Larkwell grunted. He was bent over the third and last crewman, who had been strapped in a bucket seat immediately behind the pilot. Crag moved to his side and looked down at the recumbent figure. The man's suit seemed to have withstood the terrible impact. His helmet looked intact, and his faceplate was clouded.

Prochaska nodded affirmatively. "Breathing," he said.

Crag knelt and checked the unconscious man as best he could before finally getting back to his feet.

"It's going to be a helluva job getting him back."

Larkwell's eyes opened with surprise. "You mean we're going to lug that bastard back to the Aztec?"

"We are."

Larkwell didn't reply. Crag loosened the unconscious man from his harnessing. Larkwell watched for a while before stooping to help. When the last straps were free they pulled him close to the edge of the hatch opening. Crag made a mental inventory of the cabin while Larkwell unscrewed two metal strips from a bulkhead and laced straps from the safety harnessing between them, making a crude stretcher.

Crag opened a narrow panel built into the rear bulkhead and involuntarily whistled into his lip mike. It contained two short-barreled automatic rifles and a supply of ammunition. Larkwell eyed the arms speculatively.

"Looks like they expected good hunting," he observed.

"Yeah," Crag grimly agreed. He slammed the metal panel shut and looked distastefully at the unconscious man. "I've a damned good notion to leave him here."

"That's what I was thinking."

Crag debated, and finally shrugged his shoulders. "Guess we're elected as angels of mercy. Well, let's go."

"Yeah, Florence Nightingale Larkwell," the construction boss spat. He looped a line under the unconscious man's arms and rolled him to the brink of the opening.

"Ought to shove him out and let him bounce a while," he growled.

Crag didn't answer. He ran the other end of the line around a metal stanchion and signaled Larkwell to edge the inert figure through the hatch. Crag let the line out slowly until it became slack. Larkwell straightened up and leaned against the hatch combing with a foolish look on his face. Crag took one look at his gaping expression.

"Oxygen," he snapped. Larkwell looked blank. He seized the extra cylinder from his belt and hooked it into Larkwell's suit, turning the valve. Larkwell started to sway, and almost fell through the hatch combing before Crag managed to pull him to safety.

Within moments comprehension dawned on Larkwell's face. Crag quickly checked his own oxygen. It was low. Too low. The time they had lost taking the wrong route . . . the time taken to open Bandit's hatch . . . had upset Nagel's oxygen calculations. It was something else to remember in the future. He switched cylinders, then made a rapid calculation. It was evident they couldn't carry the injured man back with the amount of oxygen remaining. He got on the interphones and outlined the problem to Nagel.

"Try one of Bandit's cylinders," he suggested. "They just might fit."

"No go. I've already looked them over." He kicked the problem around in his mind.

"Here's the routine," he told him. "You start out to meet us with a couple of extra cylinders. We'll take along a couple of Bandit's spares to last this critter until you can modify the

FIRST ON THE MOON 85

valves on his suit to fit our equipment. Prochaska can guide the works. Okay?"

"Roger," Prochaska cut in. Nagel gave an affirmative grunt.

Crag lowered two of Bandit's cylinders and the stretcher to the floor of the crater, then took a last look around the cabin. Gotch, he knew, would ask him a thousand technical questions regarding the rocket's construction, equipment, and provisioning. He filed the mental pictures away for later analysis and turned to Larkwell.

"Let's go." They descended to the plain and rolled the unconscious crewman onto the stretcher. Crag grunted as he hoisted his end. It wasn't going to be easy.

The return trip proved a nightmare. Despite the moon's low surface gravity—one-sixth that of earth—the stretcher seemed an intolerable weight pulling at their arms. They trudged slowly toward the Aztec with Crag in the lead, their feet kicking up little fountains of dust.

Before they had gone half a mile, they were sweating profusely and their arms and shoulders ached under their burden. Larkwell walked silently, steadily, but his breath was becoming a hoarse pant in Crag's earphones. The thought came to Crag that they wouldn't make it if, by any chance, Nagel failed to meet them. But he can't fail—not with Prochaska guiding them, he thought.

They reached the end of the rill and stopped to rest. Crag checked his oxygen meter. Not good. Not good at all, but he didn't say anything to Larkwell. The construction boss swung his eyes morosely over the plain and cursed.

"Nine planets and thirty-one satellites in the Solar System and we had to pick this dog," he grumbled. "Gotch must be near-sighted."

Crag sighed and picked up his end of the stretcher. When Larkwell had followed suit they resumed their trek. They were moving around the base of a small knoll when Larkwell's foot struck a pothole in the ash and he stumbled. He dropped the end of the stretcher in trying to regain his balance. It struck hard against the ground, transmitting the jolt to Crag's aching shoulders. He lowered his end of the stretcher, fearful the plow had damaged the injured man's helmet. Larkwell watched unsympathetically while he examined it.

"Won't make much difference," he said.

Crag managed a weak grin. "Remember, we're angels of mercy."

"Yeah, carrying Lucifer."

The helmet proved intact. Crag sighed and signaled to move on. They hoisted the stretcher and resumed their slow trek toward the Aztec.

Crag's body itched from perspiration. His face was hot, flushed and his heart thudded in his ears. Larkwell's breathing became a harsh rasp in the interphones. Occasionally Prochaska checked their progress. Crag thought Nagel was making damned poor time. He looked at his oxygen meter several times, finally beginning to worry. Larkwell put his fears into words.

"We'd better drop this character and light out for the Aztec," he growled. "We're not going to make it this way."

"Nagel should reach us soon."

"Soon won't be soon enough."

"Nagel! Get on the ball," Crag snapped curtly into the interphones.

"Moving right along." The oxygen man's voice was a flat imperturbed twang. Crag fought to keep his temper under control. Nagel's calm was maddening. But it was their necks that were in danger. He repressed his anger, wondering again at the wisdom of trying to save the enemy crewman. If he lived?

In short time Larkwell was grumbling again. He was on the point of telling him to shut up when Nagel appeared in the distance. He was moving slowly, stooped under the weight of the spare oxygen cylinders. He appeared somewhat like an ungainly robot, moving with mechanical steps—the movements of a machine rather than a man. Crag kept his eyes on him. Nagel never faltered, never changed pace. His figure grew steadily nearer, a dark mechanical blob against the gray ash. Crag suddenly realized that Nagel wasn't stalling; he simply lacked the strength for what was expected of him. Somehow the knowledge added to his despair.

They met a short time later. Nagel dropped his burden in the ash and squirmed to straighten his body. He looked curiously at the figure in the stretcher, then at Crag.

"Doesn't make much sense to me," he said critically. "Where are we going to get the oxygen to keep this bird alive?"

"That's my worry," Crag snapped shortly.

"Seems to me it's mine," Nagel pointed out. "I'm the oxygen man."

Crag probed the voice for defiance. There was none. Nagel was merely stating a fact—an honest worry. His temper was subsiding when Larkwell spoke.

"He's right. This bird's a parasite. We ought to heave him in the rill. Hell, we've got worries enough without . . ."

"Knock it off," Crag snarled harshly. There was a short silence during which the others looked defiantly at him.

"Stop the bickering and let's get going," Crag ordered. He felt on the verge of an explosion, wanted to lash out. Take it easy, he told himself.

With fresh oxygen and three men the remainder of the trip was easier. Prochaska was waiting for them. He helped haul the Bandit crewman to the safety of the space cabin. When it was pressurized they removed their suits and Crag began to strip the heavy space garments from the injured man's body. He finished and stepped back, letting him lie on the deck.

They stood in a tight half-circle, silently studying the inert figure. It was that of an extremely short man, about five feet, Crag judged, and thin. A thinness without emaciation. His face was pale, haggard and, like the Aztec crewmen's, covered with stubbly beard. He appeared in his late thirties or early forties but Crag surmised he was much younger. His chest rose and fell irregularly and his breathing was harsh. Crag knelt and checked his pulse. It was shallow, fast.

"I don't know." He got to his feet. "He may have internal injuries . . . or just a bad concussion."

"To hell with him," spat Larkwell.

Prochaska said, "He'll either live or die. In either case there's not much we can do about it." His voice wasn't callous, just matter-of-fact. Crag nodded agreement. The Chief turned his back. Crag was brooding over the possible complications of having an enemy in their midst when his nostrils caught a familiar whiff. He turned, startled. The Chief was holding a pot of coffee.

"I did smuggle one small helping," he confessed.

Crag looked thoughtfully at the pot. "I should cite you for a court-martial. However . . ." He reached for the cup the Chief was extending.

They drank the coffee slowly, savoring each drop, while Larkwell outlined their next step. It was one Crag had been worrying about.

"As you know, the plans call for living in the Aztec until we can get a sheltered airlock into operation," Larkwell explained. "To do that we gotta lower this baby to the horizontal so I can loosen the afterburner section and clear out the gunk. Then we can get the prime airlock installed and working. That should give us ample quarters until we can build the permanent lock—maybe in that rill we passed."

"We got to rush that," Nagel cut in. "Right now we lose total cabin pressure every time we stir out of this trap. We can't keep it up for long."

Crag nodded. Nagel was right. The airlock had to be the

first order of business. The plans called for just such a move and, accordingly, the rocket had been designed with such a conversion in mind. Only it had been planned as a short-term stopgap—one to be used only until a below-surface airlock could be constructed. Now that Drone Able had been lost—

"Golly, what'll we do with all the room?" Prochaska broke in humorously. He flicked his eyes around the cabin. "Just imagine, we'll be able to sleep stretched out instead of doubled up in a bucket seat."

Larkwell took up the conversation and they listened while he outlined the step-by-step procedure. It was his show and they gave him full stage. He suggested they might be able to use one of Aztec's now useless servo motors in the task. When he finished, Crag glanced down at the Bandit crewman. Pale blue eyes stared back at him. Ice-blue, calm, yet tinged with mockery. They exchanged a long look.

"Feel better?" Crag finally asked, wondering if by any chance he spoke English.

"Yes, thank you." The voice held the barest suggestion of an accent.

"We brought you to our ship . . ." Crag stopped, wondering how to proceed. After all the man was an enemy. A dangerous one at that.

"So I see." The voice was laconic. "Why?"

"We're human," snapped Crag brutally. The pale blue eyes regarded him intently.

"I'm Adam Crag, Commander," he added. The Bandit crewman tried to push himself up on his elbow. His face blanched and he fell back.

"I seem to be a trifle weak," he apologized. He looked at the circle of faces before his eyes settled back on Crag. "My name is Richter. Otto Richter."

Prochaska said, "That's a German name."

"I am German."

"On an Iron Curtain rocket?" Nagel asked sarcastically. Richter gave the oxygen man a long cool look.

"That seems to be the case," he said finally. The group fell silent. It was Crag's move. He hesitated. When he spoke his tone was decisive.

"We're stuck with you. For the time being you may regard yourself as confined. You will not be allowed any freedom . . . until we decide what to do with you."

"I understand."

"As soon as we modify the valves on your suit to fit our cylinders we're going to move you outside." He instructed Nagel to get busy on the valves, then turned to Larkwell.

"Let's get along with lowering this baby."

CHAPTER 10

"Gordon Nagel?" The professor turned the name over in his mind. "Yes, I believe I recall him. Let's see, that would have been about . . ." He paused, looking thoughtfully into space.

The agent said, "Graduated in '55. One of your honor students."

"Ah, yes, how could I have forgotten?" The Professor folded his hands across his plump stomach and settled back in his chair.

"I seem to recall him as sort of an intense, nervous type," he said at last. "Sort of withdrawn but, as you mentioned, quite brilliant. Now that I think of it—"

He abruptly stopped speaking and looked at the agent with a startled face.

"You mean the man in the moon?" he blurted.

"Yes, that's the one."

"Ah, no wonder the name sounded so familiar. But, of course, we have so many famous alumni. Ruthill University prides itself—"

"Of course," the agent cut in.

The professor gave him a hurt look before he began talking again. He rambled at length. Every word he uttered was taped on the agent's pocket recorder.

"Gordon Nagel, the young man on the moon flight? Why certainly I recall young Nagel," the high school principal said. "A fine student . . . one of the best." He looked archly at the agent down a long thin nose.

"Braxton High School is extremely proud of Gordon Nagel. Extremely proud. If I say so myself he has set a mark for other young men to strive for."

"Of course," the agent agreed.

"This is a case which well vindicates the stress we've put on the physical and life sciences," the principal continued. "It is the objective of Braxton High School to give every qualified student the groundwork he needs for later academic success. That is, students with sufficiently high I.Q.," he added.

"Certainly, but about Gordon Nagel . . . ?"

"Yes, of course." The principal began to speak again. The agent relaxed, listening. He didn't give a damn about the moon but he was extremely interested in the thirty some years of Nagel's life preceding that trip. Very much so. He left the school thinking that Nagel owed quite a lot to Braxton High. At least the principal had inferred as much.

"Yes, I *did* go with Gordon for a while," Mrs. LeRoy Farwell said. "But of course it was never serious. Just an occasional school dance or something. He might be famous but, well, frankly he wasn't my type. He was an awful drip." Her eyes brushed the agent's face meaningfully.

"I like 'em live, if you know what I mean."

"Certainly, Mrs. Farwell," the agent said gravely. "But about Nagel . . . ?"

There were many people representing three decades of contact with Gordon Nagel. Some of them recalled him only fleetingly. Others rambled at length. Odd little entries came to life to fit into the dossier. Photographs and records were exhumed. Gordon Nagel . . . Gordon Nagel . . .

The file on Gordon Nagel grew.

Colonel Michael Gotch didn't like the idea of an addition to the Aztec crew. Didn't like it at all. He informed Crag that the rescue had been entirely unnecessary. Unrealistic, was the word he had used. He was extremely interested in the fact that Bandit housed an arsenal. He suggested, in view of Drone Able's loss, they shouldn't overlook Bandit's supplies.

"Especially as you have another mouth to feed," he said blandly.

Crag agreed. He didn't say so but he had already planned just such a move. The Colonel immediately launched into a barrage of questions concerning the crashed rocket. He seemed grieved when Crag couldn't supply answers down to the last detail.

"Look," Crag finally exploded, "give us time . . . time. We just got here. Remember?"

"Yes . . . yes, I know. But the information is vital," Gotch said firmly. "I would appreciate it if you would try . . ."

Crag cursed and snapped the communicator off.

"What's wrong? The bird colonel heckling you?"

"Hounding is the word," Crag corrected. He fixed the Chief with a baleful eye and uttered an epithet with regard to the Colonel's ancestry. Prochaska chuckled.

Larkwell quickly demonstrated that he knew the Aztec inside and out far better than did any of the others. Aside from several large cables supplied expressly for the purpose of lowering the rocket, he obtained the rest of the equipment needed from the ship.

Under his direction two winches were set up about thirty yards from the ship and a cable run to each to form a V-line. A second line ran from each winch to a nearby shallow gully. Heavy weights—now useless parts of the ship's engines— were fastened to these and buried. The lines were intended to anchor the winches during the critical period of lowering the rocket. Finally Larkwell ran a guide line from the Aztec's nose to a third winch. This one was powered by an electric motor which was powered by the ship's batteries.

While Larkwell and Nagel prepared to lower the rocket Crag smoothed off an area of the plain's surface and marked off a twenty-foot square. He finished and looked at his handiwork with satisfaction. Richter's eyes were filled with interest.

"Using it to chart the frequency of meteorite falls," Crag explained. "We'd like to get an idea of the hazard."

"Plenty," Richter said succinctly. He started to add more and stopped. Crag felt the urge to pump him but refrained. The least he became involved the better, he thought. It didn't escape him that the German seemed to have recovered to a remarkable extent. Well, that was something else to remember. Richter injured was one thing. But Richter recovered . . .

He snapped the thought off and turned toward the base of the rocket, indicating that the German should follow. Larkwell was testing the winches and checking the cables when they arrived.

"About ready," he told Crag.

"Then let her go."

The construction boss nodded and barked a command to

Prochaska and Nagel, who were manning the restraining winches. When they acknowledged they were ready he strode to the power winch.

"Okay." His voice was a terse crack in the interphones. The Aztec shuddered on its base, teetering, then its nose began to cant downward. It moved slowly in an arc across the sky.

"Take up," Larkwell barked into the mike. The guide lines tautened.

"Okay."

This time Prochaska and Nagel fed line through the winches more slowly. The nose of the rocket had passed through sixty degrees of arc when its tail began to inch backward, biting into the plain.

"Hold up!" Larkwell circled the rocket and approached the tailfins from one side. He looked up at the body of the ship, then back at the base. Satisfied it would hold he ordered the winches started. The nose moved slowly toward the ground, swaying slightly from side to side. In another moment it lay on its belly on the plain.

"Now the real work begins," Larkwell told Crag. "We gotta clean everything out of that stovepipe and get the airlock rigged." His voice was complaining but his face indicated the importance he attached to the job.

"How long do you figure it'll take?"

Larkwell rubbed his faceplate thoughtfully. "About two days, with some catnaps and some help."

"Good." Crag looked thoughtfully at Richter. "Any reason you can't help?" he asked sharply.

"None at all," Richter answered solemnly.

"While Larkwell and Nagel labored in the tail section, Crag and Prochaska rearranged the space cabin. The chemical commode was placed in one corner and a nylon curtain rigged around it—their one concession to civilization. Crag was conscious of Richter's eyes following them—weighing, analyzing, speculating. He caught himself swiveling around at odd times to check on him, but Richter seemed unconcerned.

Electric power from the batteries was limited. For the most part they would be living on space rations—food concentrates supplemented with vitamin pills—and a square of chocolate daily per man. Later, when the airlock was installed in the area now occupied by the afterburners and machinery, they would be able to appreciably extend their living quarters. Until then, Crag thought wryly, they would live like sardines—with an enemy in their midst. An enemy and a saboteur, he mentally corrected. Aside from that there was the constant danger from meteorite falls. He shook his head despairingly. Life on the moon wasn't all it could be. Not by a damn sight.

Nagel was becoming perturbed over their oxygen consumption. He had set up the small tanks containing algae in a nutrient solution, tending them like a mother hen. In time, if the cultivation were successful, the small algae farm would convert the carbon dioxide from their respiration into oxygen. At the present time the carbon dioxide was being absorbed by chemical means. As things stood, it was necessary for the entire crew to don spacesuits every time one of them left the cabin. Each time the cabin air was lost in the vacuum of the moon. Crag pointed out there was no alternative until the airlock was completed, a fact which didn't keep Nagel from complaining.

Otto Richter recovered fast. Before another day had passed—the Aztec continued to operate by earth clock—he seemed to have completely recovered. It was evident that concussion and shock had been the extent of his injuries. Crag didn't know whether to be sorry or glad, he didn't, in fact, know what to do with the man. He gave firm orders that Richter was never to be left alone—not for a moment.

He told him: "You will not be allowed in the area of any of the electronic equipment. First time you do . . ." He looked meaningfully at him.

"I understand," the German said. Thereafter, except for occasional trips to the commode, or to help with work, he kept to the corner of the space cabin allotted him.

Larkwell came up for the evening meal wearing a grim look. He extended his hand toward Crag, holding a jagged chunk of rock nearly the size of a baseball.

Crag took the hunk and hefted it thoughtfully. "Meteorite?" The others clustered around.

"Yeah. I saw a hole in that cleared off section and reached down. There she was, big as life."

"If that had hit this pipe we'd be dead ducks," Prochaska observed.

"But it didn't hit," Crag corrected, trying to allay any gathering nervousness. "It just means that we're going to have to get going on the rill airlock as soon as possible."

"How will loss of Able affect that?" Nagel asked curiously.

"Only in the matter of size," Crag explained. The possible loss of a drone was taken into account. The plastiblocks are constructed to make any size shelter possible. We'll start immediately when Baker lands." He looked thoughtfully at the men. "Let's not borrow any trouble."

"Yeah, there's plenty without borrowing any more," Prochaska agreed. He smiled cheerfully. "I vote we all stop worrying and eat."

Another complication arose. Drone Baker would be in orbit the following morning. Prochaska had to be prepared to bring it down. He was busy moving his equipment into one compact corner opposite the commode. He rigged a curtain around it, partly for privacy but mainly to mark off a definite area prohibited to Richter.

The communicator was becoming another problem that harried Crag. A government geologist wanted a complete description of Arzachel's rock structure. A space medicine doctor had a lot of questions about the working of the oxygen-carbon dioxide exchange system. Someone else—Crag was never quite sure who—wanted an exact description of how the Aztec had handled during letdown. In the end he got on the communicator and curtly asked for Gotch.

"Keep these people off our backs until we land Drone Baker," he told him. "It's not headquarters for some damned quiz program."

"You're big news," Gotch placated. "What you tell us will help with future rockets."

"Like a mineral description of the terrain?"

"Even that. But cheer up, Commander. The worst is yet to come." He broke off before Crag could snap a reply. Prochaska grinned at his discomfiture.

"That's what comes of being famous," he said. "We're wheels."

"A wheel on the moon." Crag looked questioningly at him. "Is that good?"

"Damned if I know. I haven't been here long enough."

Crag was surprised to see how rapidly work in the tail section was progressing. Larkwell had loosened the giant engines and fuel tanks and pulled them from the ship with power from one of the rocket's servo motors. They lay on the dusty floor of the plain, incongruous in their new setting. He thought it a harbinger of things to come. A rocket garage on the floor of barren Arzachel. Four men attempting to build an empire from the hull of a space ship. In time it would be replaced by an airlock in a rill . . . a military base . . . a domed city. Pickering Field would become a transportation center, perhaps the hub of the Solar System's transportation empire. First single freighters, then ore trains, would travel the highways of space between earth mother and her long separated child. He sighed. The ore trains were a long way in the future.

Larkwell crawled out from the cavern he had hollowed in the hull and stretched. "Time for chow," he grunted. His voice over the interphones sounded tired. Nagel followed him looking morose. He didn't acknowledge Crag's presence.

At evening by earth clock they ate their scant fare. They were unusually silent. The Chief seemed weary from his long vigil on the scope. Larkwell's face was sweaty, smudged with grease. He ate quickly, with the air of a man preoccupied with weighty problems. Nagel was clearly bushed. Larkwell's fast pace had been too much for him. He wore a cross, irritable expression and avoided all conversation. Richter sat alone, seemingly unconcerned that he was a virtual prisoner, confined to one small corner of the cabin barely large enough to provide sleeping space. Crag had no feelings where he was concerned, neither resentment nor sympathy. The German was just a happenstance, a castaway in the war for Arzachel. Or, more probable, he thought, the war for the moon.

After chow the men took turns shaving with the single razor. It had been supplied only because of the need to keep the oxygen ports in the helmets free and to keep the lip mikes clear.

"Pure luxury," Prochaska said when his turn came. "Nothing's too good for the spaceman."

"Amen," Crag agreed. "I hope the next crew is going to get a bar of soap."

"For their sake I hope they pick something better than this crummy planet," Larkwell grunted.

Drone Baker had entered the moon's gravisphere at the precise time spelled out by the earth computers. Its speed had dropped to a mere two hundred miles per hour. It began to accelerate, pulled by the moon, moving in a vast

FIRST ON THE MOON

trajectory calculated to put it into a closing orbit around the barren satellite. Prochaska picked it up and followed it on the scope. Telemeter control from Alpine fired the first braking rockets. The blast countered the moon's pull. Drone Baker was still a speck on the scope—a solitary traveler rushing toward them through the void.

"Seems incredible it took us that long," Crag mused, studying the instrument panel. He reached over and activated the analog. Back on earth saucers with faces lifted to the skies were tracking the drone's flight. Their information was channeled into computer batteries, integrated, analyzed, and sent back into space. The wave train ended in a gridded scope—the analog Crag was viewing.

"Seemed a damned lot shorter when we were up there," he speculated aloud.

"That's one experience that really telescopes time," the Chief agreed. "I'd hate to have to sweat it out again."

"When do we take over?"

Prochaska glanced at the master chrono. "Not till 0810, give or take a few minutes. It depends on the final computations from Alpine."

"Better catch some sleep," Crag suggested. "It's going to be touchy once we get hold of it."

"We'll be damn lucky if we get it down in Arzachel."

"We'd better." Crag grinned. "Muff this and we might as well take out lunar citizenship."

"No thanks. Not interested."

"What's the matter, Max, no pioneer spirit?"

"Go to hell," Prochaska answered amiably.

"Now, Mr. Prochaska, that's no way to speak to your commanding officer," Crag reproved with mock severity.

"Okay. Go to hell, Sir," he joked.

Richter was a problem. Someone had to be awake at all times. Crag decided to break the crew into watches, and laid out a tentative schedule. He would take the first watch,

Larkwell would relieve him at midnight, and Nagel would take over at 0300. That way Prochaska would get a full night's sleep. He would need steady nerves come morning. He outlined the schedule to the crew. Neither Larkwell nor Nagel appeared enthusiastic over the prospect of initiating a watch regime, but neither protested openly.

When the others were asleep, Crag cut off the light to preserve battery power. He studied the lunar landscape out the port, thinking it must be the bleakest spot in the universe. He twisted his head and looked starward. The sky was a grab bag of suns. Off to one side giant Orion looked across the gulf of space at Taurus and the Pleiades, the seven daughters of Atlas.

CHAPTER 11

"COMMANDER!" Crag came to with a start. Prochaska was leaning over him. Urgency was written across his face.

"Come quick!" The Chief stepped back and motioned with his head toward the instrument corner. Crag sprang to his feet with a sense of alarm. Richter and Larkwell were still asleep. He glanced at the master chrono, 0610, and followed him into the electronics corner. Nagel was standing by the scope, a frightened look on his face.

"What's up?"

"Nagel woke me at six. I came in to get ready for Drone Baker . . ."

"Get to the point," Crag snapped irritably.

"Sabotage." He indicated under the panel. "All the wiring under the main console's been slashed."

Crag felt a sense of dread. "How long will it take to make repairs?"

"I don't know—don't know the full extent of the damage."

"Find out," Crag barked. "How about the communicator?"

"Haven't tried it," Prochaska admitted. "I woke you up as soon as I found what had happened." He reached over and turned a knob. After a few seconds a hum came from the console. "Works," he said.

"See how quickly you can make repairs," Crag ordered. "We've got to hook onto the drone pretty quick."

He swung impatiently toward Nagel. "Was anyone up during your watch? Did anyone go to the commode?"

Nagel said defensively: "No, and I was awake all the time." Too defensive, Crag thought. But no one had stirred during his watch. Therefore, the sabotage had occurred between midnight and the time Nagel wakened Prochaska. But, wait . . . Prochaska could have done the sabotage in the few moments he was at the console after Nagel woke him. It would have taken just one quick slash—the work of seconds. That left him in the same spot he'd been in with regard to the time bomb.

He grated harshly at Nagel: "Wake Larkwell and get on with the airlock. And don't chatter about what's happened," he added.

"I won't," Nagel promised nervously. He retreated as if glad to be rid of Crag's scrutiny.

"A lousy mess," Prochaska grunted.

Crag didn't answer.

"If we don't solve this, we're going to wind up dead," he pursued.

Crag turned and faced him. "It could be anybody. You . . . me."

"Yeah, I know." The Chief's face got a hard tight look. "Only it isn't . . . it isn't me."

"I don't know that," Crag countered.

Prochaska said bitterly: "You'd better find out."

"I will," Crag said shortly. He got on the communicator. It took several minutes to raise Alpine. He wasn't surprised when Gotch answered, and briefly related what had happened.

"Is there any possibility of telemetering her all the way in?" He knew there wasn't, but he asked anyway.

"Impossible."

"Okay, we'll try and make it from here."

The Colonel added a few comments. They were colorful but definitely not complimentary. He got the distinct impression the Colonel wasn't pleased with events on the moon. When his cold voice faded from the communicator, Crag tried the analog. The grid scope came to life but it was blank. Of course, he thought, Drone Baker was cut off from earth by the body of the moon. It could not be simulated on the analog until it came from behind the blind side where the earth saucers could track its flight.

"Morning," Larkwell said, sticking his head around the curtain. "How about climbing into your suits so we can get out of this can?" Crag studied his face. It seemed void of any guile. Nagel stood nervously behind him.

"Okay," Crag said shortly. He hated to have Prochaska lose the precious moments. They hurriedly donned their suits and Nagel decompressed the cabin, Larkwell opened the hatch and they left. Crag closed it after them and released fresh oxygen into the cabin. Richter took off his suit and returned to his corner. His eyes were bright with interest. He knows, Crag thought.

At 0630 the communicator came to life. A voice at the other end gave Drone Baker's position and velocity as if nothing had happened. The drone, on the far side of the moon, was decelerating, dropping as servo mechanisms operating on timers activated its blasters. It was guided solely by the radio controlled servos, following a flight path previously determined by banks of computers. Everything was in apple-pie order, except for the snafu in Arzachel, Crag thought bitterly.

Prochaska worked silently, swiftly. Crag watched with a helpless feeling. There wasn't room for both of them to work at one time. The Chief's head and arms literally filled the opening of the sabotaged console. Once he snapped for more light and Crag beamed a torch over his shoulder, fretting from the inaction.

Sounds came through the rear bulkhead where Larkwell and Nagel were working in the tail section. Strange, Crag thought, to all appearances each crew member was a dedicated man. But one was a traitor. Which one? That's what he had to find out. Richter would have been the logical suspect were it not for the episode of the time bomb. No, it hadn't been the German. It was either the competent Prochaska, the sullen Nagel or the somehow cheerful but inscrutable Larkwell. But there should be a clue. If only he knew what to look for. Well, he'd find it. When he did . . . He clenched his fists savagely.

At 0715 Alpine simulated the drone on the analog. Fifteen minutes later Prochaska pulled his head from the console and asked Crag to try the scope. It worked.

"Now if I can get those damn wires that control the steering and braking rockets . . ." He dived back into the console. Crag looked at the chrono, then swung his eyes to the instruments. Drone Baker was coming in fast. The minutes ticked off. The communicator came to life with more data. Baker was approaching Ptolemaeus on its final leg. The voice cut off and Gotch came on.

"We're ready to transfer control."

Prochaska shook his head negatively without looking up.

"What's the maximum deadline?" Crag asked.

"0812, exactly three minutes, ten seconds," Gotch rasped. Prochaska moved his head to indicate maybe. The communicator was silent. Crag watched the master chrono.

At 0812 Prochaska was still buried in the panel. Crag's dismay grew—dismay and a sense of guilt over the sabotage. Gotch had warned him against the possibility innumerable times. Now it had happened. The loss of Drone Able had been a bad blow; the loss of Baker could be fatal, not only to the success of their mission but to their survival.

Survival meant an airlock and the ability to live on their scant supplies until Arzachel was equipped to handle incoming rockets on a better-than-chance basis. Well, one thing at a time, he thought. He suppressed the worry nagging at his mind. Just now it was Drone Baker's turn at bat.

At 0813 Prochaska sprang to his feet and nodded. Crag barked an okay into the communicator while the Chief got his bearings on the instruments. Crag hoped the lost minute wouldn't be fatal. By 0814 Prochaska had the drone under control. It was 90,000 feet over Alphons traveling at slightly better than a thousand miles per hour. He hit the braking rockets hard.

"We're not going to make it," he gritted. He squinted his eyes. His face was set, grim.

"Hold it with full braking power."

"Not sufficient fuel allowance."

"Then crash it as close as possible."

Prochaska nodded and moved a control full over. The drone's braking rockets were blasting continuously. Crag studied the instruments. It was going to be close. By the instrument data they couldn't make it. Drone Baker seemed doomed. It was too high, moving too fast despite the lavish waste of braking power. His hand clenched the back of Prochaska's seat. He couldn't tear his eyes from the scope. Baker thundered down.

Suddenly the drone was on them. It cleared the north rim of Arzachel at 3,000 feet. Too high, Crag half-whispered. The difference lay in the lost minute. Prochaska pushed and held the controls. Crag pictured the rocket, bucking, vibrating, torn by the conflict of energies within its fragile body.

Prochaska fingered the steering rockets and pushed the drone's nose upward. Crag saw it through the port. It rushed through space in a skidding fashion before it began to move upward from the face of the moon. Prochaska hit the braking jets with full power. Crag craned his head to follow its flight. Out of one corner of his eye he saw Nagel and Larkwell on the plain, their helmeted heads turned skyward. He scrunched his face hard against the port and caught the drone at the top of its climb.

It was a slender needle with light glinting on its tail— the Sword of Damocles hanging above their heads. It hung . . . suspended in space . . . then began backing down, dropping stern first with flame and white vapor pouring from its tail jets. It came fast. Occasional spurts from radial jets around its nose kept its body perpendicular to the plain. Vapor from the trail fluffed out hiding the body of the rocket. The flame licked out while the rocket was still over a hundred feet in the air.

Prochaska cursed softly. The rocket seemed riveted to the black sky for a fraction of a second before it began to fall. Faster . . . faster. It smashed into the lunar surface, lost from sight.

"Exit Baker," Prochaska said woodenly. Quietly Crag got on the communicator and reported to Gotch. There was a brief silence when he had finished.

Finally Gotch said, "Drone Charlie will be launched on schedule. We'll have to reassess our logistics, though. Maybe we'd better knock off the idea of the airlock-in-the-gully idea and shoot along extra oxygen and supplies instead. How does the meteorite problem look?"

"Lousy," said Crag irritably. "We've had a scary near miss. I wouldn't bet on being able to survive too long in the open. Again there was a silence.

"You'll have to," Gotch said slowly, "unless you can salvage Baker's cargo."

"We'll check that."

"You might investigate the possibility of covering the Aztec with ash."

"Sure . . . sure," Crag broke in. "Good idea. I'll have the boys break out the road grader immediately."

"Don't be facetious," Gotch reprimanded. "We have a problem to work out."

"You're telling me!"

"In the meantime, try and clean up that other situation."

By "other situation" Crag knew he was referring to the sabotage. Sure, be an engineer, intelligence agent, spaceman and superman, all rolled into one. He wrinkled his face bitterly. Still he had to admire the Colonel's tenacity. He was a man determined to conquer the moon.

"Will do," Crag said finally. "In the meantime we'll look Baker over. There might be some salvage."

"Do that," the Colonel said crisply. He cut off.

CHAPTER 12

"Max Prochaska was a real well-liked boy," Mrs. Arthur Bingham said firmly, "friendly with everyone in town. Of course, Vista was just a small place then," she added reminiscently. "Not like now, especially since the hellicopter factory moved in. I do declare, a soul wouldn't recognize the place any longer, with all the housing tracts and the new supermarket—"

"Certainly," the agent interjected, "but about Max Prochaska."

"Yes, of course." Mrs. Bingham bit her lip reflectively. "My husband always said Max would go places. I wish he could have lived to see it." For just a moment her eyes brimmed wetly, then she blew her nose, wiping them in the process. The agent waited until she had composed herself.

"Little Max—I always think of him as Little Max," she explained—"was smart and pleasant, real well liked at school. And he *always* attended church." She stressed the word always.

"Just think, now they say he's on the moon." Her eyes fixed the agent with interest. "You'd think he'd get dizzy."

The agent almost enjoyed tracing Max Prochaska's history. It was a neat, wrapped-up job, one that moved through a regular sequence. Teacher . . . minister . . . family doctor . . . druggist . . . scoutmaster . . . athletic director—all the ties a small-town boy makes and retains. Everything was clear-cut, compact. Records, deeds, acquaintances—all in one handy package. The memory of a man who grew up in a small town persisted, borne in the minds of people whose worlds were small. The Vista paper had obligingly carried Prochaska's biography, right on the front page, under the headline: VISTAN LANDS ON MOON. The leading local drugstore was featuring a Prochaska sundae and the Mayor of the town had proclaimed MAX PROCHASKA week.

Clearly, Vista was proud of its native son, but not nearly as proud as the elderly couple who still tended a chicken ranch on the outskirts of town.

"Max is a good boy," Mrs. Prochaska said simply. Her husband beamed agreement.

On the surface, Prochaska's record seemed clean—a good student, well-liked, the usual array of girls, and nothing much in the way of peccadillos you could hang a hat on. The agent's last view of the town was a sign at the city limits: VISTA—THE HOME OF MAX PROCHASKA.

Drone Baker looked a complete loss. It had smashed tail down onto the ash covered plain about four miles to the southeast of the Aztec, off the eastern lip of the curved crescent Prochaska had dubbed "Backbone Ridge."

Crag calculated that the positions of Bandit, the drone and their own rocket roughly formed an equilateral triangle on the floor of the crater. The lower section of the rocket was crushed, its hull split lengthwise.

Crag and Larkwell studied the scene from a small knoll. The drone lay in a comparatively level area about thirty feet from the edge of a deep fissure, carreened at a steep angle from the vertical. Only its tail imbedded into the ground kept it from toppling.

"Might as well have a closer look," Larkwell said finally. Crag nodded and beckoned Richter, who was waiting at the bottom of the knoll. Since the sabotage incident he had split the crew into two sections which varied according to task. Richter was used by either section as needed. It wasn't an arrangement that Crag liked but he didn't feel it wise, or safe, to allow anyone the privilege of privacy.

Richter circled the base of the knoll and met them. When they reached the rocket, Larkwell circled it several times, studying it from all angles.

"We might come out pretty well," he said finally. His voice carried a dubious note. He lifted his head and contemplated the rocket again. "Maybe some of the cargo rode through."

"We hope," Crag said.

"I wouldn't bank too much on it."

"Think we might get inside?"

Larkwell said decisively: "Not this boy. Not until we pull the nose down. This baby's ready to topple."

They were discussing their next move when Prochaska came in on the interphone: "Alpine wants the dope on Baker."

Damn Alpine, Crag thought moodily. He contemplated the rocket. "Tell 'em it's still here." All at once he felt depressed. Strain, he told himself. Since blast-off his life had been a succession of climaxes, each a little rougher than the one preceding. Not that he was alone in his reactions. His mind switched to Nagel. The oxygen man had become sullen, irritable, almost completely withdrawn from the group. He was, Crag thought, a lonely, miserable man. Even Larkwell was beginning to show the affects of their struggle to survive. His normal easygoing manner was broken by periods of surliness. Only Prochaska had managed to maintain his calm approach to life, but the effects were telling physically. His face was a mask of parchment drawn tightly over bone, accentuating his tired hollow eyes.

But Richter seemed to be thriving. Why not? He was a doomed man given a fresh reprieve on life, with no responsibilities to burden his existence. He was on a gravy train for the time being. Still, Richter was in an unenviable spot. Nagel was openly hostile toward him. His demeanor and looks were calculated to tell the German he was an undesirable intruder. Larkwell's attitude was one of avoidance. He simply acted as if the German were not on the moon. When in the course of work it became necessary to give Richter an order, he did it with a short surly bark. Prochaska concealed whatever feeling he had toward the German. No, he thought, Richter's lot wasn't easy.

He tried to push the mood aside. It wouldn't push. He checked his oxygen, and decided to swing over to Bandit before returning. The sooner they got started on the salvage job, the better. He communicated his plan to the others.

Larkwell protested, "Getting ready to open this baby's more imporant. We'll never get started on the airlock fooling around this god forsaken desert."

"We'll get to that, too," Crag promised, fighting to keep his temper under control. "By going from here we'll save a couple of miles over having to make a special trip."

"Suit yourself," the construction boss said truculently.

Crag nodded stiffly and started toward the enemy rocket, now lost to view behind intervening rock formations. By unspoken agreement Larkwell fell in at the rear, leaving Richter sandwiched between them. The German lived constantly under the scrutiny of one or another of the crew. Crag intended to keep it that way.

The trip was more difficult than he had anticipated. Twice they were forced to detour around deep fissures. Before they had gone very far Crag's radiation counter came to life. He made a note of the spot thinking that later they would map the boundaries of the radioactive area. Once or twice he checked his course with Prochaska. His oxygen meter told him they would have to hurry when they topped a low knoll of glazed rock and came upon the ship.

He stopped and turned, watching Richter. If he had expected any show of emotion he was disappointed. His face was impassive. It gave Crag the feeling that he wasn't really seeing the rocket—that he was looking far beyond, into nothingness. His eyes behind the face plate were vacuous pools.

"We didn't have time to bury your companions," Crag said matter-of-factly. He indicated the rocket with a motion of his head and his voice turned cruel:

"They're still in there."

Richter's expression remained unchanged. "It doesn't

make much difference here," he said finally. He turned and faced Crag.

"One thing you should understand. They," he swept his arm toward Bandit, "were the military."

"And you?"

Richter said stiffly: "I am a scientist."

"Who destroyed our drone thinking it was us." They faced each other across the bleak lunar desert. The German's eyes had become blue fires—azure coals leaping into flame.

"It makes no difference what you think," he said after a moment. "My conscience is clear."

"Nuts." Larkwell spat the word with disgust. Richter shrugged and turned back toward the rocket. Crag looked at him with varying emotions. One thing was sure, he thought. Richter was a cool customer. He had seen new depths in his blue eyes when they had faced each other. They were hard eyes, ablaze with ice . . . the eyes of a fanatic—or a saint. He pushed the thought aside.

Prochaska came in on the phones to inquire about their oxygen. Crag checked, chagrined to find that it was too low to spend more than a few minutes at the rocket. He opened the arms locker, thinking he would have to get rid of the weapons. They could be dangerous in the wrong hands. He had been unable to carry them back the first trip. Then he had regarded them as something totally useless on the moon. Now he wasn't so sure.

He hurriedly studied the space cabin, seeking the information Gotch had requested. The floor and walls were heavily padded with some foam material—standard procedure to absorb vibration and attenuate noise. Aside from the controls, there were no projecting metal surfaces or hard corners . . . the view ports were larger . . . acceleration pads smaller, thicker. All in all, the cabins of the two rockets were quite similar. He was examining the contents of the supply cabinets when Larkwell reminded him of their diminishing oxygen supply. They hurriedly plundered Bandit of six oxygen cylinders and started back across Arzachel's desolate plain.

Crag arbitrarily broke the lunar day into twenty-four hour periods to correspond with earth time. Twelve hours were considered as "day," the remaining time as "night." He set up regular communication periods in order to schedule their activities. Under the arrangement Alpine came in promptly at exactly a half-hour before breakfast—0500 by earth clock —and again following the evening meal. Prochaska monitored the channel during the workday to cover possible urgent messages. The schedule allowed a twelve-hour work period during the day and a three-hour work period following the evening meal, from 7:00 to 10:00. The communication periods quickly deteriorated into routine sessions—a good omen to Crag—but Gotch kept his finger in the pie. Crag had the satisfaction of knowing he was available around the clock. Consequently, when the communicator came to life midway through the regular twelve-hour work period, he knew something was brewing—something he wasn't going to like. So did Prochaska. His voice, when he called Crag to the communicator, spelled trouble.

Crag used the ear microphones for privacy and acknowledged the call with a distinct feeling of unease. As he had expected, the caller was Gotch.

"Drone Charlie was launched at 0600," he told Crag. "We'll feed you the data on the regular channels." There was a brief silence. "This one's got to make it," he added significantly.

Crag said stonily: "We'll do our best."

"I know you will, Commander. I have absolutely no fear on that score. How's everything going?" The twangy voice across the abyss of space took on a solicitous tone that set his nerves on edge. Something's wrong—something bad, he thought. The Colonel sounded like a doctor asking a dying patient how he felt.

"Okay, everything seems in hand. We've got the ship in good shape and Larkwell thinks we might fare pretty well with the drone. It might be in better shape than we first thought."

"Good, good, glad to hear it. We need a silver lining once in a while, eh?"

"Yeah, but I'm fairly certain you didn't call just to cheer me up," Crag said dryly. "What's on your mind?" The silence came again, a little longer this time.

CHAPTER 13

"YOU'RE IN TROUBLE." Gotch spoke like a man carefully choosing his words. "Intelligence informs us that another rocket's been fired from east of the Caspian. BuNav's got a track on it."

Crag waited.

"There are two possibilities," Gotch continued. "The first and most logical assumption is that it's manned. We surmise that from the fact that their first manned rocket was successful—that is, as far as reaching the moon is concerned. The assumption is further borne out by its trajectory and rate of acceleration." His voice fell off.

"And the second possibility?" Crag prompted.

"Warhead," Gotch said succinctly. "Intelligence informs us that the enemy is prepared to blow Arzachel off the face of the moon if they fail to take it over. And they have failed —so far." Crag tossed the idea around in his mind.

He said fretfully, "I doubt if they could put a warhead down on Arzachel. That takes some doing. Hell, it's tough enough to monitor one in from here, let alone smack from earth."

"I think you're right, but they can try." Gotch's voice became brisk. "Here's the dope as we see it. We think the rocket contains a landing party for the purpose of establishing a moon base. In Arzachel, naturally, because that's where the lode is."

"More to the point, you expect an attack on Pickering Base," Crag interjected.

"Well, yes, I think that is a reasonable assumption. . . ."

Crag weighed the information. Gotch was probably right. A nuclear explosion on the moon would be detected on earth. That was the dangerous course—the shot that could usher in World War III and perhaps a new cave era

Attack by a landing party seemed more logical. They batted ideas back and forth. The Colonel suggested that just before the landing phase of Red Dog—the code name assigned the new rocket—Crag post armed guards at some point covering the Aztec.

"Might as well get some use out of Bandit's automatic weapons," Gotch dryly concluded.

Crag disagreed. He didn't think it likely that any attack would take the form of a simple armed assault. "That would give us time to get off a message," he argued. "They can't afford that."

Gotch pointed out that neither could they launch a missile while still in space. "A homing weapon couldn't differentiate between Aztec, Baker and Bandit," he said

"But they'd still have to have some sure fire quick-kill method," Crag insisted.

"You may be right. Have you a better plan?"

Crag did, and outlined it in some detail. Gotch listened without comment until he had finished.

"Could work," he said finally. "However, it's going to shoot your schedule, even if you could do it."

"Why can't we?"

"You're not supermen, Commander," he said tersely. "The psychiatrists here inform us that your crew—as individuals—should be near the breaking point. We know the cumulative strain. To be truthful with you, we've been getting gray hair over that prospect."

"Nuts to the psychiatrists," Crag declared with a certainty he didn't feel. "Men don't break when their survival depends on their sanity."

"No?" The single word came across the void, soft and low.

"We can do it," Crag persisted.

"All right, I agree with the plan. I think you're wrong but you're the Commander in the field." His voice was flat. "Good luck." He cut off abruptly.

Crag looked at the silent panel for a moment. Another problem, another solution required. Maybe Gotch was right. Maybe they'd all wind up as candidates for the laughing academy—if they lived long enough. The thought didn't cheer him. Well, he'd better get moving. There was a lot to be done. He looked up and saw the question in Prochaska's eyes. Might as well tell him, he thought.

He repeated the information Gotch had given, together with his plan. Prochaska listened quietly, nodding from time to time. When he finished, they discussed the pros and cons of Crag's proposed course of action. Prochaska thought it would work. In the end they decided to pursue the plan without telling the others the full story. It might be the breaking point, especially for Nagel, and they would be needing a good oxygen man in the coming days. Crag got on the interphone and called Larkwell, who was working in the tail section with the others.

"Judging from what you've seen of Bandit, how long would it take to make it livable as crew quarters?"

"Why?" he asked querulously.

"I haven't time to go into that now," Crag said evenly. "Just give me your best estimate."

"You can't make it livable. It's hot."

"Not that hot. You've just got the radiation creeps. Let's have the estimate."

Larkwell considered a moment. "There's quite a weld job on the hull, assuming we could get the necessary patch metal from Bandit. We'd have to haul one helluva lot of gear across that damned desert—"

"How long?" Crag cut in.

"Well, three days, at least. But that's a minimum figure."

"That's the figure you'll have to meet," Crag promised grimly. "Start now. Use Nagel and Richter. Load up the gear you'll need and get in a trip before chow."

"Now?" Larkwell's voice was incredulous. "What about winding up this job first? The airlock is damned important."

"Drop it," Crag said briefly. There was silence at the other end of the interphone.

"Okay," the construction boss grumbled finally.

Crag suggested that Prochaska make the first trip with them to look over Bandit's electronic gear. He would need to know what repairs and modifications would be necessary to make it usable. The Chief was delighted. It would mark the first time he'd been out of the space cabin since the day of their landing.

Crag watched them leave through the port. It was impossible to tell the crew members apart in their bulky garments. The extra oxygen and the tools Larkwell had selected gave them an odd shambling gait, despite the low gravity. They plodded in single file, winding slowly across the plain. The thought struck him that they resembled grotesque life forms from some alien planet. For just a moment he felt sorry, and a trifle guilty, over assigning

Nagel to the trip. The oxygen man was already in a state of perpetual fatigue. Still, he couldn't allow anyone the luxury of rest. Work was in the cards—grueling, slavish toil if they were to survive.

It struck Crag that this was a moment of great risk. Of the four figures plodding toward Bandit, one was an enemy . . . one a saboteur. Yet, what could either accomplish by striking now? Nothing! *Not while I live*, he thought. Strangely enough, Richter bothered him more than the saboteur. There was a quality about the man he couldn't decipher, an armor he couldn't penetrate. It occurred to him that, outwardly at least, Richter was much like Prochaska—quiet, calm, steady. He performed the tasks assigned him without question . . . evinced no hostility, no resentment. He was seemingly oblivious to Nagel's barbs and Larkwell's occasional surly rebuffs. On the face of the record he was an asset—a work horse who performed far more labor than Nagel.

He decided he couldn't write the German off as a factor to be continually weighed—weighed and watched. He was no ordinary man. Of that he was sure. Richter's presence on the enemy's first moon rocket was ample testimony of his stature. What were his thoughts? His plans? What fires burned behind his placid countenance? Crag wished he knew. One thing was certain. He could never lower his guard. Not for a second.

He sighed and turned away from the viewport. A lot of data had piled up. He'd give Alpine a little work to do to get Gotch off his neck. He reached for the communicator thinking of Ann. Probably got someone else lined up by now, he thought sourly.

Work on Bandit progressed slowly. Nagel dragged through each successive work shift on the verge of exhaustion. Crag expected him to collapse momentarily. His disintegration took him further and further from the group. He ate silently, with eyes averted. He didn't protest the arduous hours, but the amount of work he performed was negligible. Larkwell maintained his stamina but had become more quiet in the process. He seldom smiled . . . never joked. Occasionally he was truculent or derisive, referring to Bandit as the "Commander's hot box."

Richter remained impersonal and aloof, but performed his assigned tasks without apparent resentment. Crag noticed that he stayed as far from Larkwell as possible, perhaps fearing violence from the burly construction boss. Prochaska, alone, maintained a cheerful exterior—for which Crag was thankful.

He was watching them now—the evening of the last day of Larkwell's three-day estimate—returning from the Bandit. The four figures were strung out over half a mile. He regarded that as a bad omen. They no longer worked as a crew, but as separate individuals, each in his separate world, with exception of Prochaska. He turned away from the port with the familiar feeling that time was running out, and mentally reviewed what remained to be done.

Making Bandit habitable was a must. There still remained the arduous task of transferring their belongings and gear to Bandit. Drone Baker had to be toppled and her cargo salvaged. Then there was Drone Charlie, at present just a minute speck somewhere in the great void between earth and her moon; but in somewhat less than forty-eight hours it would represent tons of metal hurtling over the rim of Arzachel. This time they couldn't fumble the ball. The building of the airlock in the rill loomed in the immediate future —an oppressive shadow that caused him no end of worry. There were other problems, too—like the item of Red Dog . . . the possible battle for control of the moon.

Red Dog, in particular, had become the prime shadow darkening Arzachel's ashy plains. He thought about the emotional deterioration which had laid an iron grip over the expedition and wondered if they could hang on through the rough days ahead. All in all, the task of colonizing the moon appeared an extremely formidable one. He shook off his apprehensions and began planning his next step.

That evening Crag knocked off the usual three hour work period following evening chow. Nagel tumbled onto his pad and was asleep almost instantly. His breathing was a harsh rasp. At Crag's suggestion Prochaska took the watch until midnight. Crag stood guard the remainder of the night to allow Nagel and Larkwell a full night's rest.

While the others slept, Crag brooded at the port. Once he ran his hand over his face, surprised at the hardness. All bone and no flesh, he thought. He looked toward the north wall of Arzachel.

In a few short hours Drone Charlie would come blazing over the rim, and Red Dog snapping at its heels.

CHAPTER 14

"ADAM CRAG was not a God-fearing man," the minister stated. His tone implied that Crag had been just the opposite. "Not a bit like his parents. The best family guidance in the world, yet he quit Sunday school almost before he got started. I doubt that he's ever been to church since."

He looked archly at the agent. "Perhaps a godless world like the moon is just retribution."

A garage mechanic, a junk dealer and the proprietor of a tool shop had a lot to say about Adam Crag. So did the owner of a small private airport. They remembered him as a boy with an insatiable appetite for tearing cars apart and converting them to what the junk dealer termed "supersonic jalopies."

Many people in El Cajon remembered Adam Crag. Strangely enough, his teachers all the way back through grade school had little difficulty in recalling his antics and attitudes. An elementary teacher explained it by saying, "He was that kind of a boy."

The family doctor had the most to say about Adam. He had long since retired, a placid seventyish man who had elected to pass his last years in the same house, in an older section of the town, in which he'd been born.

He sat swinging and talking, reminiscing about "the growing up of young Adam," as he put it. The agent had made himself at home on the front steps, listening. The doctor's comments were little short of being an eulogy.

He finished and was silent, tapping a black briar pipe against his hand while he contemplated the agent with eyes which had long since ceased to see.

"One other thing," he added finally. "Adam was sure a heller with the girls."

The agent started to comment that Crag's dossier looked like the roll call of a girl's dormitory but refrained. He didn't want to prejudice the testimony.

Zero hour on the plains of Arzachel. The sun, an intolerably brilliant ball pasted against the ebony sky, had started its drop toward the horizon. The shadows on the plain were lengthening, harbingers of the bitter two-weeks-long night to come. They crept out from the sheer wall of the crater, reaching to engulf Pickering Base with icy fingers.

Crag and Prochaska were alone, now, in the stripped cabin of the Aztec. Nagel and Richter, under Larkwell's command, had departed for Bandit an hour earlier with the last of their supplies. Crag disliked splitting the crew but saw no alternative. He had to gamble. The element of certainty, the ability to predict, the expectations of logic—all these had vanished, swept away by the vagaries of chance. They could do only so much. Beyond that their fate was pawn to the chaotic cross fires of human elements pitted against the architecture of the cosmos. They were puppets in the last lottery of probability.

Prochaska broke the silence: "It's going to be close."

Crag's eyes remained riveted to the instruments. Drone Charlie and Red Dog were plunging through space separated by a scant half-hour's flight time. Despite the drone's long launch lead, the gap between the two rockets had been narrowed to a perilous point. Drone Charlie was decelerating rapidly, her braking rockets flaring spasmodically to slow her headlong flight.

"We'd better get into our suits," Crag said finally. "We want to get out of this baby the second Charlie lets down."

Prochaska nodded. They left their suits unpressurized for the time being to allow full mobility. In the moments ahead Prochaska, in particular, couldn't afford to be hampered by the rigidity the suit possessed when under pressure.

They turned back to the control panel. Charlie was hurtling over Alphons, dropping toward the bleak lunar landscape with incredible speed. The mechanical voice from Alpine droned a stream of data. There was a rapid exchange of information between Prochaska and Alpine. At its conclusion he began taking over control of the drone. Crag watched tensely. Prochaska's fingers, even though encased in the heavy suit material, moved with certainty. In a little while he spoke without looking up.

"Got it," he said laconically. He studied the instruments, then his fingers sought the buttons controlling Charlie's forward braking rockets.

Crag thought: *This is it*. Within scant moments the drone

had covered the sky over the tangled land lying between Alphons and Arzachel. It swept over the brimming cliffs at a scant two thousand feet. He saw the rocket through the forward ports. White vapor flared from its nose rockets. The Chief had it under full deceleration. The cloud of vapor covered its body. Prochaska moved the steering control and the rocket slanted upward at ever-increasing angle of climb. Crag strained his neck to keep it in sight. He thought its rate of climb was too rapid but Prochaska seemed unperturbed. His calm approach to the problem of landing the drone gave Crag renewed confidence.

All at once, it seemed, Drone Charlie was hanging high in the sky, a tapered needle miraculously suspended in the heavens. Then it began dropping . . . dropping. Bursts of smoke and white vapor shot from its tail jets, becoming continuous as the rocket hurtled toward the plain. The drone was lost to sight in its own clouds, but he charted its progress by the vapor spurts at its lower edge. Prochaska was draining the tail braking jets of every ounce of energy. Suddenly the rocket gave the illusion of hanging in mid-air. The gap between it and the stark terrain below seemed to have stopped closing. Crag half expected the blasting stern tubes to begin pushing the drone back into the sky. But . . . no! It was moving down again, slowly.

Prochaska moved another control. A servo-mechanism within the rocket stirred to life and a spidery metal network moved out from its tail housing. The drone dropped steadily, ever slower, and finally settled. The shock-absorbing frame folded, was crushed. At the same instant Prochaska silenced its rockets. It settled down, its tail tubes pushed into the plain's powdery ash scarcely a mile from the Aztec.

"Perfect." Prochaska sounded pleased with himself. His thin face broke into a satisfied smile.

"Nice going," Crag agreed. "Now let's get out of this trap."

His eyes lingered for an instant on the analog. Red Dog had already cleared Ptolemaeus. He snapped his face plate shut, clicked on the interphone and turned the oxygen valve. His suit began to swell and grow rigid against his body. When they were pressurized, he opened the hatch and they clambered out onto the plain. He closed the hatch behind them and struck off in the direction of Bandit with the Chief at his heels.

They moved as rapidly as possible. Their feet in the heavy insulated space boots kicked up small fountains of dust which dropped as quickly as they rose. From time to time Crag looked back toward the brimming cliffs. Prochaska plodded head down. His quickened breathing in the interphones sounded harsh to Crag. Plainly the long hours of monitoring the Aztec's instruments had made him soft. The microphone in his helmet came to life. It was Larkwell.

"Red Dog's cleared the rim," he told them.

Crag glanced back. His eyes caught the wispish trail of white vapor high above the cliffs before he saw the rocket itself. It was already in vertical attitude, letting down amid a cloud of white vapor from its stern braking rockets.

"All hands disconnect their interphones," he commanded. "From here on out we operate in silence." The Red Dog interphone system might or might not be on the same band they used. He wasn't about to take that risk.

"Okay," Larkwell acknowledged. "We're shutting off."

Crag remembered that the German's interphones were still connected. Slip one. He decided to leave his own open—at least he'd be forewarned if anyone tried to alert the Red Dog crew. He turned back toward the rocket. Red Dog was dropping about two or three miles from the Aztec in the direction of the wrecked Baker.

White smoke and flame poured from its stern tubes. It slowed visibly as it neared the lunar surface. He thought that a plumb bob dropped through the long axis of the rocket would form a right angle with the surface of Arzachel. Pilot's good, he thought. He watched until it touched down teetering on its stern tubes for a moment before coming to rest; then he turned and hurried to overtake Prochaska.

The Chief's face behind his mask was covered with perspiration. He panted heavily. Crag beckoned him to follow and moved behind a low swale of rock where they would be safe from detection. The nose of Bandit jutted into the sky about a mile ahead of them. He motioned toward it, gesturing for Prochaska to go on. The Chief nodded understanding and struck off.

Crag turned and began climbing a low rocky ridge that now lay between him and Red Dog. He stopped just below its crest and searched for a safe vantage point. To his right a serrated rock structure extended up over the backbone of the ridge. He angled toward it, then followed the outcropping to a point where he could see the plain beyond. Red Dog had its tail planted in the ash about three miles distant.

Minute figures milled at its base, small blobs of movement against the crater floor. No sounds broke the silence of Crag's open interphones. He took this as a sign that the Red Dog sets operated on a different band. But he couldn't be sure. The tremendous advantage of having communication with his own men must be discarded.

His vigil was rewarded a few moments later when the blobs around Red Dog's base began moving in the direction of the Aztec. It struck him that they couldn't see the rocket from their present position due to small intervening hillocks, although both Baker and Charlie were clearly visible. He decided the Aztec's horizontal position had tipped them to its identity while they were still space-borne. One of the Red Dog crewmen, obviously the leader, drew ahead of his companions. The other two seemed to be struggling with some object they carried between them. They moved close together, halting from time to time. He returned his gaze

FIRST ON THE MOON . 125

to the rocket, conjecturing that another crewman would have remained behind. If so, he was in the space cabin. The ship seemed lifeless. The landing party approached a small ridge overlooking the Aztec, bringing them closer to his lookout.

He saw that the two men following the leader were having difficulty with their burden. They walked slowly, uncertainly, pausing from time to time. The lead man started up the rocky knoll overlooking the Aztec. His movements were slow, wary. He crouched near the top of the ridge, scanning the plain beyond before waving to his companions to follow. The gesture told Crag that their interphones were disconnected. The crewmen near the base of the knoll started climbing, moving with extreme difficulty. He watched them, wondering, until they reached the leader. They stood for a moment scouting the plain, then two of the men crouched over the burden they had lugged up the knoll.

A weapon, Crag guessed. He tried to discern its shape but failed. A few moments later one of the men stepped back. A puff of white rose from the knoll. A trail of vapor shot toward the Aztec. A portable rocket launcher! His eyes tracked the missile's flight. The vapor trail terminated at its target. An instant later the Aztec disintegrated. Black chunks of the rocket hurtled into the lunar skies, becoming lost to sight. Within seconds only a jagged few feet of broken torn metal marked the site of man's first successful landing on the moon. *Wow, what a weapon,* he thought. It didn't merely push a hole in the Aztec. It disintegrated it, completely. That was one for Gotch. He filed the thought away and watched.

The figures on the knoll searched the scene for a long time. Finally they turned and started back, carrying the rocket launcher with them. The act of saving the weapon told him that Red Dog carried more rockets than just the single shot fired—a disconcerting thought.

He cautiously withdrew from his post and picked his way down the ridge toward Bandit, moving as rapidly as the rough terrain permitted. Everything now depended on the next move of the Red Dog's crew, he thought. One thing was certain—there would be no quarter shown. The ruthless destruction of the Aztec had set the pattern for the coming battle of Arzachel. It was a declaration of war with all rules of human warfare discarded. Well, that was okay with him.

He was breathing heavily by the time he reached a spot overlooking Bandit. Nagel had decompressed the cabin and they were waiting for him with the hatch open. He crossed the clearing and a moment later was in the space cabin. He watched the gauge until it was safe to cut off his suit pressure and open his face plate. He looked at Richter; his face was blank. Tersely, then, he related what had happened.

"I sort of expected that," Prochaska said quietly when he had finished. "It was the logical way."

"Logical to attempt to murder men?" Nagel asked bitterly.

"Entirely logical," Crag interjected. "The stakes are too big for a few human lives to matter. At least we've been warned."

He turned to Prochaska. "Disconnect Richter's mikes until this show's over."

The Chief nodded. Richter stood quietly by while his lip microphone was disconnected and withdrawn from the helmet. Nagel's face showed satisfaction at the act, but Larkwell's expression was wooden.

Crag said, "Defense of Bandit will be under Prochaska's command." He looked grimly at his second-in-command. "Your fort has one automatic rifle. Make it count if you have to use it." The Chief nodded.

Larkwell spoke up, "How about you?"

"I'll be scouting with the other automatic rifle. Stay in your suits and keep ready. If they start to bring up the rocket launcher I'll signal. If that happens you'll have to get out of here, pronto. You'd better check your oxygen," he added as an afterthought.

"If they think we're dead ducks they won't be toting the launcher," Prochaska said.

"We hope." Crag exchanged his oxygen cylinder for a fresh one, then checked one of the automatic rifles, slipping two extra clips in his belt. On second thought he hooked a spare oxygen cylinder to the back straps. He nodded to Nagel, snapped his face plate shut and pressurized his suit. When the cabin was decompressed, he opened the hatch, scanning the knoll carefully before descending to the plain. He struck off toward the ridge overlooking Red Dog. The ground on this side of the spur was fairly flat and he made good time, but was panting heavily by the time he reached his lookout point on the crest.

CHAPTER 15

CRAG SIGHTED the Red Dog party immediately—three figures plodding in single file toward Drone Baker. He saw with satisfaction that they had discarded the rocket launcher. He took that as a sign they believed the Aztec crew dead. He found a halfway comfortable sitting position, and settled back to await developments.

The distant figures moved across the plain with maddening slowness. From time to time he returned his eyes to the enemy rocket. It showed no signs of life. Once he debated taking the gamble of trying to reach it, but as quickly discarded the idea. Caught on the open plain and he'd be a gone gosling.

He waited.

After what seemed a long while, the invaders reached a point overlooking Drone Baker. One of the figures remained on a small rise overlooking the drone while the other two separated and approached it from different directions. The tactic disquieted him. It indicated that the newcomers were not entirely convinced that they were alone in Crater Arzachel.

After another interminably long time, the two figures approaching the rocket met at its base. They walked around the rocket several times, then struck out, this time toward Drone Charlie. Their companion left his lookout point and cut across the plain to join them.

Crag squirmed uncomfortably. He was tired and hungry; his muscles ached from the constriction of the suit. His body was hot and clammy, and perspiration from his brow stung his eyes. He sighed, wishing he had a cigarette. Strange, he hadn't smoked in over a year but all at once the need for tobacco seemed overwhelming. He pushed the thought aside.

The invaders were strung out in single file, moving in a direction which brought them closer to his position. He shifted to a point below the crest, moving slowly to avoid detection. Their path crossed his field of vision at a distance of about half a mile. At the closest point he saw they carried rifles in shoulder slings. He took this as another indication they suspected the presence of survivors. The invaders stopped and rested at a point almost opposite him. He fidgeted, trying to get his body into a more comfortable position.

Finally they resumed their trek. Before they reached the drone they halted. One man remained in the cover of a spur of rock while the other two separated and advanced on the drone from different directions. Crag cursed under his breath. They certainly weren't going to be sitting ducks. Perhaps it was just a precaution. Simply good infantry tactics, he told himself, but it still raised a complication.

He waited. The two invaders closed on the drone, meeting at its base. They evidently decided it was abandoned, for they left within a few minutes walking to join their waiting companion. After a short huddle they struck out in the direction of Bandit. This was the move he had waited for.

He withdrew to the lee side of the ridge and picked his way toward Bandit as rapidly as possible, taking care not to brush against the sharp slivers of rock. He drew near the rocket, thinking that the open hatch would be a dead giveaway. Still, there was no alternative. A fort without a gunport was no fort at all. He climbed to a spot close to the crest of the ridge and peered back in the direction of the invaders, startled to find they were nearer than he had supposed. He hastily withdrew his head, deciding it was too late to warn the others to abandon the rocket. If the invaders climbed straight up the opposite side of the ridge, they conceivably could catch his crew on the open plain. That made another complication.

He scanned the ridge. Off to his right a series of granite spurs jutted from the base rock in finger formation. He picked his way toward them, then descended until he found shelter between two rock outcroppings which gave him a clear view of Bandit. He checked his automatic rifle, moving the control lever to the semi-automatic position. The black rectangle that marked Bandit's hatch seemed lifeless.

He waited.

Long minutes passed. He cursed the eternal silence of the moon which robbed him of the use of his ears. A cannon could fire within an inch of his back and he'd never know it, he thought. He moved his head slightly forward from time to time in an effort to see the slope behind him. Nothing happened. His body itched intolerably from perspiration. He readjusted the suit temperature setting, gaining a slight respite from the heat. All at once he caught movement out of the corner of his face plate and involuntarily jerked his head back. He waited a moment, aware that his heart was pounding heavily, then cautiously moved forward. One of the invaders was picking his way down the slope in a path that would take him within thirty yards of his position. The man moved slowly, half-crouched, keeping his rifle cradled across his arm.

They know, he thought. The open hatch was the giveaway. He anxiously searched Bandit. No sign of life was visible. He gave silent thanks that the invaders had not lugged their rocket launcher with them. Prochaska, he knew, would be watching, crouched in the shadow of the hatch opening behind the heavy automatic rifle. He estimated the distance between the base of the slope and the rocket at 400 yards—close enough for Prochaska to pick off anyone who ventured onto the plain.

He waited while the invader passed abreast of him and descended to the base of the plain, taking cover in the rocks. He halted there and looked back. A few moments later Crag saw the second of the invaders moving down the slope about a hundred yards beyond his companion. He, too, stopped near the base of the rocks. Where was the third man? The same technique they used before, Crag decided. He would be covering his companions' advance from the ridge. That made it more difficult.

He studied the two men at the edge of the plain. It looked like a stalemate. They either had to advance or retreat. Their time was governed by oxygen. If they advanced, they'd be dead pigeons. Prochaska couldn't miss if they chose to cross the clearing. As it was, neither side could get a clear shot at the distance separating them, although the invaders could pour a stream of shells into the open hatch. But Prochaska would be aware of that danger and would have taken refuge to one side of the opening, he decided. There was another complication. The shells were heavy enough to perforate the rocket. Well, he'd worry about that later. He moved his head for a better view of the invaders.

The man nearest him had gotten into a prone position and was doing something with the end of his rifle. Crag watched, puzzled. Suddenly the man brought the rifle to his shoulder, and he saw that the end of the muzzle was bulged. Rifle grenade! Damn, they'd brought a regular arsenal. If he managed to place one in the open hatch, the Bandit crew was doomed. Heedless of the other two Red Dog crewmen, he stepped out between the shoulders of rock to gain freedom of movement and snapped his own weapon to his shoulder. He had trouble fitting his finger into the trigger guard. The enemy was spraddled on his stomach, legs apart, adjusting his body to steady his weapon.

Crag moved his weapon up, bringing the prone man squarely into his sights. He squeezed the trigger, feeling the weapon jump against his padded shoulder, and leaped back into the protective cover of rock. Something struck his face plate. Splinter of rock, he thought. The watcher on the ridge hadn't been asleep. He dropped to his knees and crawled between the rock spurs to gain a new position. The sharp needle fragments under his hands and knees troubled him. One small rip and he'd be the late Adam Crag. He finally reached a place where he could see the lower end of the ridge.

The man he'd shot was a motionless blob on the rocky floor, his arms and legs pulled up in a grotesque fetal position. The vulnerability of human life on the moon struck Crag forcibly. A bullet hole anywhere meant sudden violent death. A hit on the finger was as fatal as a shot through the heart. Once air pressure in a suit was lost a man was dead —horribly dying within seconds. A pinhole in the suit was enough to do it. His eyes searched for the dead man's companions. The ridge and plain seemed utterly lifeless. Bandit was a black canted monolith rising above the plain, seeming to symbolize the utter desolation and silence of Crater Arzachel. For a moment he was fascinated. The very scene portended death. It was an eery feeling. He shook it off and waited. He was finally rewarded by movement. A portion of rock near the edge of the plain seemed to rise—took shape. The dead man's companion had risen to a kneeling position, holding his rifle to his shoulder.

Crag raised his gun, wondering if he could hold the man in his sights. A hundred and fifty yards to a rifleman clothed in a cumbersome space suit seemed a long way. Before he could pull the trigger, the man flung his arms outward, clawing at his throat for an instant before slumping to the rocks. It took Crag a second to comprehend what had happened. Prochaska had been ready.

A figure suddenly filled the dark rectangle of Bandit, pointing toward the ridge behind Crag. He apparently was trying to tell him something. Crag scanned the ridge. It seemed deserted. He turned toward Bandit and motioned toward his faceplate. The other understood. His interphones crackled to life. Prochaska's voice was welcome.

"I see him," he broke in. "He's moving up the slope to your right, trying to reach the top of the ridge. Too far for a shot," he added.

Crag scrambled into a clearing and scanned the ridge, just in time to see a figure disappear over the skyline. He started up the slope in a beeline for the crest. If he could reach it in time, he might prevent the sniper from crossing the open plain which lay between the ridge and Red Dog. Cops and robbers, he thought. Another childhood game had suddenly been recreated, this time on the bleak plain of an airless alien crater 240,000 miles from the sunny Southern California lands of his youth.

Crag reached the ridge. The plain on the other side seemed devoid of life. In the distance the squat needle that was Red Dog jutted above the ashy plain, an incongruous human artifact lost on the wastelands of the moon. Only its symmetry distinguished it from the jagged monolithic structures that dotted this end of the crater floor. He searched the slope. Movement far down the knoll to his right caught his eye. The fugitive was trying to reach a point beyond range of Crag's weapon before cutting across the plain. He studied the terrain. Far ahead and to the left of the invader the crater floor became broken by bizarre rock formations of Backbone Ridge—a great half-circle which arced back toward Red Dog. He guessed that the fantastic land ahead was the fugitive's goal.

He cut recklessly down the opposite slope and gained the floor of the crater before turning in the direction he had last seen the invader. He cursed himself for having lost sight of him. Momentarily, he slowed his pace, thinking he was ripe for a bushwhacking job. His eyes roved the terrain. No movement, no sign of his quarry. He moved quickly, but warily, attempting to search every inch of the twisted rock formations covering the slope ahead. His eye detected movement off to one side. At the same instant a warning sounded in his brain and he flung himself downward and to the side, hitting the rough ground with a sickening thud. He sensed that the action had saved his life. He crawled between some rock outcroppings, hugging the ground until he reached a vantage point overlooking the area ahead. He waited, trying to search the slope without exposing his position. Minutes passed.

He tossed his head restlessly. His eyes roved the plain, searching, attempting to discern movement. No movement— only a world of still life-forms. The plain—its rocks and rills—stretched before him, barren and endless. Strange, he thought, there should be vultures in the sky. And on the plain creosote bushes, purple sage, cactus . . . coyotes and rattlesnakes.

But . . . no! This was an other-world desert, one spawned in the fires of hell—a never-never land of scalding heat and unbelievable cold. He thought it was like a painting by some mad artist. First he had sketched in the plain with infinite care—a white-black, monotonous, unbroken expanse. Afterward he had splashed in the rocks, painting with wild abandon, heedless of design, form or structure, until the plain was a hodgepodge of bizarre formations. They towered, squatted, pierced the sky, crawled along the plain like giant serpents—an orgy in rock without rhyme or reason. Somewhere in the lithic jungle his quarry waited. He would flush him out.

He thought that the sniper must be getting low on oxygen. He couldn't afford to waste time. He had to reach Red Dog soon—if he were to live. Crag checked his oxygen meter and began moving forward, conscious that the chase would be governed by his oxygen supply. He'd have to remember that.

He reached a clearing on the slope just as the sniper disappeared into the rock shadows on the opposite side. He hesitated. Would the pursued man be waiting . . . covering the trail behind him? He decided not to chance crossing it and began skirting around its edge, fretting at the minutes wasted. His earphones crackled and Prochaska's voice came, a warning through the vacuum:

"Nagel says your oxygen must be low."

He glanced at the indicator on his cylinder. Still safe. He studied the rocks ahead and told Prochaska:

"I've got to keep this baby from reaching Red Dog."

"Watch yourself. Don't go beyond the point of no return." Prochaska's voice held concern.

"Stop worrying."

Crag pushed around the edge of the clearing with reckless haste. It was hard going and he was panting heavily long before he reached the spot where he had last seen the sniper.

He paused to catch his breath. The slope fell away beneath him, a miniature kingdom of jagged needle-sharp rock. There was no sign of the fugitive. The plain, too, was devoid of life. He descended to the edge of the clearing and picked his way through the debris of some eon-old geologic catastrophe. Ahead and to the left of the ridge, the plain was broken by shallow rills and weird rock outcroppings. Farther out Backbone Ridge began as low mounds of stone, becoming twisted black stalagmites hunched incongruously against the floor of the crater, ending as jagged sharp needles of rock curving over the plain in a huge arc.

A moment later he caught sight of his quarry. The invader had cut down to the edge of the plain, abandoning the protection of the ridge, making a beeline for the nearest rock extrusion on the floor of the crater. Too far away for a shot. Crag cursed and made a quick judgment, deciding to risk the open terrain in hopes of gaining shelter before the sniper was aware of his strategy.

He abandoned the protection of the slope and struck out in a straight line toward the distant mounds on the floor of the crater, keeping his eyes on the fugitive. They raced across the clearing in parallel paths, several hundred yards apart. The sniper had almost reached the first rocks when he glanced back. He saw Crag and put on an extra burst of speed, reaching the first rocks while Crag was still a hundred yards from the nearest mound. Crag dropped to the ground, thankful that it was slightly uneven. At best he'd make a poor target. He crawled, keeping his body low, tossing his head in an effort to shake the perspiration from his eyes.

"How you doing, skipper?" It was Prochaska. Lousy, Crag thought. He briefed him without slowing his pace.

The ashy plain just in front of him spurted in little fountains of white dust. He dropped flat on his belly with a gasp.

"You all right?"

"Okay," Crag gritted. "This boy's just using me for target practice." Prochaska's voice became alarmed. He urged him to retreat.

"We can get them some other way," he said.

"Not if they once get that launcher in operation. I'm moving on." There was a moment of silence.

"Okay, skipper, but watch yourself." His voice was reluctant. "And watch your oxygen. "

"Roger." He checked his gauge and hurriedly switched to the second cylinder. Now he was on the last one. The trick would be to stretch his oxygen out until the chase was ended—until the man ahead was a corpse.

He clung to the floor of the crater, searching for shelter. The ground rose slightly to his right. He crawled toward the rise, noting that the terrain crested high enough to cut his view of the base of the rocks. Satisfied that he was no longer visible, he began inching his way toward the nearest mounds.

CHAPTER 16

CRAG STUDIED the scene. He lay at one end of the great crescent of rock forming Backbone Ridge, the other end of which ended about half a mile from Red Dog. The floor of the crater between the rocket and the nearest rock formations was fairly level and unbroken. The arced formation itself was a veritable jungle of rocks of every type—gnarled, twisted rock that hugged the ground, jutting black pinnacles piercing the sky, bizarre bubble formations which appeared like weird ebony eskimo cities, and great fantastic ledges which extruded from the earth at varying angles, forming black caves against their bases.

Whole armies could hide there, he thought. Only the fugitive couldn't hide. Oxygen was still the paramount issue. He'd have to thread his way through the terrible rock jungle to the distant tip of the crescent, then plunge across the open plain to the rocket if he hoped to survive. The distance between the horns of the crescent appeared about three miles. He pondered it thoughtfully, then got on the interphones and outlined his plan to Prochaska.

"Okay, I know better than to argue," the Chief said dolefully when he had finished. "But watch your oxygen." Damn the oxygen, Crag thought irritably. He studied the labyrinth of rock into which his quarry had vanished, then rose and started across the plain in a direct line for the opposite tip of the crescent.

The first moments were the hardest. After that he knew he must be almost out of range of the sniper's weapon. Perhaps, even, the other had not seen his maneuver. He forced himself into a slow trot, his breath whistling in his ears and his body sodden inside his suit. Perspiration stung his eyes, his leg muscles ached almost intolerably, and every movement seemed made on sheer will power. The whimsical thought crossed his mind that Gotch had never painted this side of the picture. Nor was it mentioned in the manual of space survival.

He was thankful that the plain between the two tips of the crescent was fairly even. He moved quickly, but it was a long time before he reached the further tip of the crescent. He wondered if he had been observed from Red Dog. Well, no matter, he thought. He had cut the sniper's sole avenue of escape. Victory over his quarry was just a matter of time, a matter of waiting for him to appear. He picked a vantage point, a high rocky ledge which commanded all approaches to his position. After briefing Prochaska, he settled back to wait, thinking that the fugitive must be extremely low on oxygen.

Long minutes passed. Once or twice he thought he saw movement among the rocks and started to lift his rifle; but there was no movement. Illusions, he told himself. His eyes were playing him tricks. The bizarre sea of rocks confronting him was a study in black and white—the intolerable light of sun-struck surfaces contrasting with the stygian blackness of the shadows. His eyes began to ache and he shifted them from time to time to shut out the glare. He was sweating again and there was a dull ache at the back of his head. Precious time was fleeing. He'd have to resolve the chase—soon.

All at once he saw movement that was not an illusion. He half rose, raising his rifle when dust spurted from the ground a few feet to his left. He cursed and threw himself to the ground, rolling until he was well below the ridge. One thing was certain: the sniper had the ridge well under control. The Red Dog watcher must have warned him, he thought. He looked around. Off to one side a small rill cut through the rocks running in the sniper's general direction. He looked back toward the ridge, hesitated, then decided to gamble on the rill. He moved crablike along the side of the slope until he reached its edge and peered over. The bottom was a pool of darkness. He lowered himself over the edge with some misgivings, searching for holds with his hands and feet. His boot unexpectedly touched bottom.

Crag stood for a moment on the floor of the rill. His body was clothed in black velvet shadows but it was shallow enough to leave his head in the sunlight. He moved cautiously forward, half expecting the sniper to appear in front of him. His nerves were taut, edgy.

Relax, boy, you're strung like a violin, he told himself. *Take it easy.*

A bend in the rill cut off the sun leaving him in a well of blackness. He hadn't counted on that. Before he'd moved another dozen steps he realized the rill wasn't the answer. He'd have to chance getting back into the open. More time was lost. He felt the steep sides until he located a series of breaks in the wall, then slung his rifle over his shoulder and inched upward until his head cleared the edge. The sun's sudden glare blinded him. Involuntarily he jerked his head sideways, almost losing his hold in the process. He clung to the wall for a moment before laboriously pulling his body over the edge.

He lay prone against the rocks, half-expecting to be greeted by a hail of bullets. He waited quietly, without moving, then carefully raised his head. Off to one side was a series of mounds. He crawled toward them without moving his belly from the ground. When he reached the first one, he half rose and scuttled forward until he found a view of the twisted rocks where he had last seen the sniper.

The scene ahead was a still-life painting. It seemed incongruous that somewhere among the quiet rocks death moved in the form of a man. He decided against penetrating further into the tangle of rocks. He'd wait. He settled back, conscious that time was fleeing.

"Skipper, are you checking your oxygen?" The Chief's voice rattled against his eardrums. It was filled with alarm.

"Listen, I have no time—" Crag started to growl. His words were clipped short as his eyes involuntarily took the reading of his oxygen gauge. Low . . . low. He calculated quickly. He was well past the point of no return—too low to make the long trip back to Bandit. He was done, gone, a plucked gosling. He had bought himself a coffin and he'd rest there for all eternity—boxed in by the weird tombstones of Crater Arzachel. Adam Crag—the Man in the Moon.

He grinned wryly. Well, at least his quarry was going with him. He wouldn't greet his Maker empty handed. He tersely informed Prochaska of his predicament, then recklessly moved to a high vantage point and scanned the rocks beyond.

He had to make every second count. Light and shadow . . . light and shadow. Somewhere in the crisscross of light and shadow was a man-form, a blob of protoplasm like himself, a living thing that had to be stamped out before the last of his precious oxygen was gone. He was the executioner. Somewhere ahead a doomed man waited in the docks . . . waited for him to come. They were two men from opposite sides of the world, battling to death in Hell's own backyard. Only he'd win . . win before he died.

He was scanning the rocky tableau when the sniper moved into his field of vision, far to one side of Crag's position. He was running with short choppy steps, threading between the rocks toward Red Dog. His haste and apparent disregard of exposing himself puzzled Crag for a moment, then he smiled grimly. Almost out of oxygen, he thought. Well, that makes two of us. But he still had to make sure his quarry died. The thought spurred him to action.

He turned and scrambled back toward the tip of Backbone Ridge to cut the sniper's escape route. He reached the end rocks and waited. A few moments later he sighted a figure scrambling toward him. He raised his rifle thinking it was too far for a shot, then lowered it again. The sniper began moving more slowly and cautiously, then became lost to sight in a maze of rock outcroppings.

Crag waited impatiently, aware that precious moments were fleeing. He was afraid to look at his gauge, plagued by the sense of vanishing moments. Time was running out and eternity was drawing near—near to Adam Crag as well as the sniper. The rocks extended before him, a kaleidoscopic pattern of black and white. Somewhere in the tortuous labyrinth was the man he had to kill before he himself died. He watched nervously, trying to suppress the tension pulling at his muscles. A nerve in his cheek twitched and he shook his head without removing his eyes from the rocks ahead. Still there was no sign of the other.

Who was the stalker and who was the stalked? The question bothered him. Perhaps even at that instant the sniper was drawing bead. Then he'd be free to reach Red Dog —safety.

Crag decided he couldn't wait. He'd have to seek the other out, somehow flush him from cover. He looked around. Off to one side a shelf of black rock angled incongruously into the sky. Its sides were steep but its top would command all approaches to the tip of the crescent. He made his way to the base of the shelf and began scrambling up its steep sides, finding it difficult to manage toe and hand holds. He slipped from time to time, hanging desperately on to keep himself from rolling back to the rocks below. Just below the top he rested, panting, fighting for breath, conscious of his heart thudding in his ears. He had to hurry!

Slowly, laboriously he pulled himself up the last few feet and lay panting atop the shelf, none too soon. The sniper scrambled out of the rocks a scant hundred yards from Crag's position. He raised his rifle, then hesitated. The Red Dog crewman had fallen to his hands and knees and was fighting to rise. He pushed his hands against the plain in an attempt to get his feet under him. Crag lowered his rifle and watched curiously.

The sniper finally succeeded in getting to his feet. He stood for a moment, weaving, before moving toward Crag's shelf with a faltering zigzag gait. Crag raised the rifle and tried to line the sights. He had difficulty holding the weapon steady. He started to pull the trigger when the man fell again. Crag hesitated. The sniper floundered in the ash, managed to pull himself half-erect. He weaved with a few faltering steps and plunged forward on his face.

Crag watched for a moment. There was no movement. The black blob of the suit lay with the stillness of the rocks in the brazen heat of the crater. So that's the way a man dies when his oxygen runs out, he thought. He just plops down, jerks a little and departs, with as little ceremony as that. He grinned crookedly, thinking he had just watched a rehearsal of his own demise. He watched for a moment longer before turning his face back toward the plain.

Red Dog was a bare half-mile away—a clear level half-mile from the tip of Backbone Ridge. That's how close the sniper had come to living. He mulled the thought with a momentary surge of hope. Red Dog? Why not? If he could shoot his way into the space cabin he'd live . . . live. The thought galvanized him to action.

He slung his rifle over his shoulder and scrambled down the slope heedless of the danger of ripping his suit. He could make it. He had to make it! He gained the bottom and paused to catch his breath before starting toward the rocket. A glance at his oxygen meter told him that the race was futile. Still, he forced his legs into a run, threading through the rocks toward the floor of the crater. He reached the tip of the crescent panting heavily and plunged across the level floor of the plain. His legs were leaden, his lungs burned and sweat filled his eyes, stinging and blurring his vision. Still he ran.

The rocket rose from the crater floor, growing larger, larger. He tried to keep in a straight path, aware that he was moving in a crazy zigzag course.

The rocket loomed bigger . . . bigger. It appeared immense. Caution, he told himself, there's an hombre up there with a rifle. He halted, feeling his body weave, and tried to steady himself. High up in the nose of Red Dog the hatch was a dancing black shadow—black with movement. He pulled the rifle from his shoulder and moved the control to full automatic, falling to his knees as he did so. Strange, the ashy floor of the crater was erupting in small fountains just to his side. Danger, he thought, take cover. The warning bells were still ringing in his brain as he slid forward on his stomach and tried to steady his weapon. Dust spurted across his face plate. The black rectangle of the hatch danced crazily in his sights. He pulled back on the trigger, feeling the heavy weapon buck against his shoulder, firing until the clip was empty. His fingers hurriedly searched his belt for the spare clips. Gone. Somehow he'd lost them. He'd have to rush the rocket.

He got to his feet, weaving dizzily, and forced his legs to move. Once or twice he fell, regaining his feet with difficulty.

He heard a voice. It took him a minute to realize it was his own. He was babbling to Prochaska, trying to tell him . . .

The sky was black. No, it was white, dazzling white, white with heat, red with flame. He saw Red Dog with difficulty. The rocket was a hotel, complete with room clerk. He laughed inanely. A Single, please. No, I'll only be staying for the night. He fell again. This time it took him longer to regain his feet. He stumbled . . . walked . . . stumbled. His eyes sought the rocket. It was weaving, swaying back and forth. Foolish, he thought, there was no wind in Crater Arzachel. No air, no wind, no nothing. Nothing but death. Wait, there was someone sitting on top of the rocket—a giant of a man with a long white beard. He watched Crag and smiled. He reached out a hand and beckoned. Crag ran. The sky exploded within his brain, his legs buckled and he felt his face plate smash against the ashy floor. For all eternity, he thought. The blackness came.

Adam Crag opened his eyes. He was lying on his back.

Above him the dome of the sky formed a great black canopy sprinkled with brilliant stars. His thoughts, chaotic memories, gradually stabilized and he remembered his mad flight toward Red Dog.

This couldn't be death, he thought. Spirits didn't wear space suits. He sensed movement and twisted his head to one side. Gordon Nagel! The oxygen man's face behind the heavy plate was thin, gaunt, but he was smiling. Crag thought that he had never seen such a wonderful smile. Nagel's lips crinkled into speech:

"I was beginning to wonder when you'd make it." Even his voice was different, Crag thought. The nasal twang was gone. It was soft, mellow, deep with concern. He thought it was the most wonderful sound he had ever heard.

"Thanks, Gordon," he said simply. He spoke the words thinking it was the first time he'd ever addressed the other by his first name.

"How'd you ever locate me?"

"Started early," Nagel said. "I was pretty sure you'd push yourself past the point of no return. You seemed pretty set on getting that critter."

"It's a wonder you located me." He managed to push himself to a sitting position.

"Prochaska didn't think I could. But I did. Matter of fact, I was pretty close to you when you broke from the rocks heading for Red Dog." Red Dog! Crag twisted his head and looked toward the rocket.

"He's lying at the base of the rocket," Nagel said, in answer to his unspoken question. "Your last volley sprayed him."

"Skipper!" Prochaska's voice broke impatiently into his earphones.

"Still alive," Crag answered.

"Yeah—just." Prochaska's voice was peevish. "You were lucky with that last burst of fire."

"Thanks to my good marksmanship," Crag quipped weakly.

"I wish you'd quit acting like a company of Marines and get back here."

"Okay, Colonel."

Prochaska cursed and Crag grinned happily. It was good to be alive, even in Crater Arzachel.

Nagel helped him to his feet and Crag stood for a moment, feeling the strength surge back into his body. He breathed deeply, luxuriating in the plentiful oxygen. Fresh oxygen. Fresh as a maiden's kiss, he thought. Oxygen was gold. More than gold. It was life.

"Ready, now?"

"Ready as I ever will be," Crag answered. "Lead on, Gordon."

They had almost reached Bandit when Crag broke the silence. "Why did you come . . . to the moon, Gordon?"

Nagel slowed his steps, then stopped and turned.

"Why did you come, Commander?"

"Because . . . because . . ." Crag floundered. "Because someone had to come," he blurted. "Because I was supposed to be good in my field." His eyes met Nagel's. The oxygen man was smiling, faintly.

"I'm good in mine, too," he said. He chewed at his bottom lip for a moment.

"I could give the same reasons as you," he said finally. "Truthfully, though, there's more to it." He looked at Crag defiantly.

"I was a misfit on earth, Commander. A square peg in a round hole. I had dreams . . . dreams, but they were not the dreams of earth. They were dreams of places in which there were no people." He gave an odd half-smile. "Of course I didn't tell the psych doctors that."

"There's plenty I didn't tell 'em, myself," Crag said.

"Commander, you might not understand this but . . . I

like the moon." He looked away, staring into the bleakness of Arzachel. Crag's eyes followed his. The plain beyond was an ash-filled bowl broken by weird ledges, spires, grotesque rocks. In the distance Backbone Ridge crawled along the floor of the basin, forming its fantastic labyrinths. Yet . . . yet there was something fascinating, almost beautiful about the crater. It was the kind of a place a man might cross the gulfs of space to see. Nagel had crossed those gulfs. Yes, he could understand.

"I'll never return to earth," he said, almost dreamily.

"Nonsense."

"Not nonsense, Commander. But I'm not unhappy at the prospect. Do you remember the lines:

Under the wide and starry sky
Oh, dig the grave and let me lie . . .

Well, that's the way I feel about the moon."

"You'll be happy enough to get back to earth," Crag predicted.

"I won't get back, Commander. Don't want to get back." He turned broodingly toward Bandit.

"Maybe we'd better move on," Crag said gently. "I crave to get out of this suit."

CHAPTER 17

"MARTIN LARKWELL was a good boy," the superintendent said reminiscently, "and of course we're highly pleased he's made his mark in the world." He looked at the agent and beamed. "Or should I say the moon?" The agent smiled dutifully.

FIRST ON THE MOON

"Young Martin was particularly good with his hands. Not that he wasn't smart," he added hurriedly. "He was very bright, in fact, but he was fortunate in that he coupled it with an almost uncanny knack of using his hands."

The superintendent rambled at length. The agent listened, thinking it was the same old story. The men in the moon were all great men. They had been fine, upstanding boys, all bright with spotless records. Well, of course that was to be expected in view of the rigorous weeding out program which had resulted in their selections. Only one of them was a traitor. Which one? The question drummed against his mind.

"Martin wasn't just a study drudge," the superintendent was saying. "He was a fine athlete. The star forward of the Maple Hill Orphanage basketball team for three years," he added proudly. He leaned forward and lowered his voice as if taking the agent into his confidence.

"We're conducting a drive to build the orphanage a new gym. Maybe you can guess the name we've selected for it?"

"The Martin Larkwell Gymnasium," the agent said drily.

"Right." The superintendent beamed. "That's how much we think of Martin Larkwell."

As it turned out, the superintendent wasn't the only one who remembered Martin Larkwell with fondness. A druggist, a grocer, a gas station operator and a little gray lady who ran a pet shop remembered the orphan boy with surprising affection. They and many others. That's the way the chips fall, the agent thought philosophically. Let a man become famous and the whole world remembers him. Well, his job was to separate the wheat from the chaff.

In the days to follow he painstakingly traced Martin Larkwell's trail from the Maple Hill Orphanage to New York, to various construction jobs along the East Coast and, finally, through other agents, to a two-year stint in Argentina as construction boss for an American equipment firm. Later the trail led back to America and, finally, to construction foreman on Project Step One. His selection as a member of the Aztec Crew stemmed from his excellent work and construction ability displayed during building of the drones. All in all, the agent thought, the record was clear and shiny bright.

Martin Larkwell, Gordon Nagel, Max Prochaska, Adam Crag—four eager scrub-faced American boys, each outstanding in his field. There was only one hitch. Who was the traitor?

Crag filled Gotch in on the latest developments in Crater Arzachel. The Colonel listened without interruption until he was through, then retaliated with a barrage of questions. What was the extent of the radioactive field? What were the dimensions of Red Dog? Had any progress been made toward salvaging the cargo of Drone Baker? How was the airlock in the rill progressing? Would he please describe the rocket launcher the enemy had used to destroy the Aztec? Crag gritted his teeth to keep from exploding, barely managing civil replies. Finally he could hold it no longer.

"Listen," he grated, "this is a four-man crew, not a damn army."

"Certainly," Gotch interrupted, "I appreciate your difficulties. I was just—in a manner of speaking—outlining what has to be done."

"As if I didn't know."

The Colonel pressed for his future plans. Crag told him what he thought in no uncertain terms. When he finished he thought he heard a soft chuckle over the earphones. Damn Gotch, he thought, the man is a sadist. The Colonel gave him another morsel of information—a tidbit that mollified him.

Pickering Field, Gotch informed him, was now the official name of the landing site in Crater Arzachel. Furthermore, the Air Force was petitioning the Joint Chiefs to make it an official part of the U.S. Air Force defense system. A fact which had been announced to the world. Furthermore, the United States had petitioned the U. N. to recognize its sovereignty over the moon. Before cutting off he added one last bit of information, switching to moon code to give it.

"*Atom job near completion,*" he spelled out. For the moment Crag felt jubilant. An atom-powered space ship spelled complete victory over the Eastern World. It also meant Venus . . . Mars . . . magical names in his mind. Man was on his way to the stars. MAN—the peripatetic quester. For just an instant he felt a pang of jealousy. He'd be pinned to his vacuum while men were conquering the planets. Or would he? But the mood passed. Pickering Field, he realized, would play an important role in the future of space flight. If it weren't the stars, at least it was the jump-off. In time it would be a vast Air Force Base housing rockets instead of stratojets. Pickering Base—the jump-off—the road to the stars. Pretty soon the place would be filled with rank so high that the bird colonels would be doing mess duty. But right now, he was Mr. Pickering Field, the Man with the Brass Eyeballs.

While the others caught up on their sleep, Crag and Prochaska reviewed their homework, as the Chief had dubbed their planning sessions. The area in which Bandit rested was too far from the nearest rill to use as a base of operation, and it was also vulnerable to meteorite damage. Bandit had to be abandoned, and soon. Red Dog would be their next home. There was also the problem of salvaging the contents of Drone Baker and removing the contents of Drone Charlie. Last, there was the problem of building the airlock in one of the rills. When they had laid out the problems, they exchanged quizzical glances. The Chief smiled weakly.

"Seems like a pretty big order."

"A very big order," Crag amended. "The first move is

to secure Red Dog." They talked about it until Crag found his eyelids growing heavy. Prochaska, although tired, volunteered to take the watch. Crag nodded gratefully—a little sleep was something he could use.

Red Dog was squat, ebony, taper-nosed, distinguishable from the lithic structures dotting this section of Crater Arzachel only by its symmetry. The grotesque rock ledges, needle-sharp pinnacles and twisted formations of the plain clearly were the handiwork of a nature in the throes of birth, when volcanoes burst and the floor of the crater was an uneasy sea of white-hot magmatic rock. Red Dog was just as clearly the creation of some other-world artificer, a creature born of the intelligence and patience of man, structured to cross the planetary voids. Yet it seemed a part of the plain, as ancient as the brooding dolomites and diorites which made the floor of Arzachel a lithic wonderland. The tail of Red Dog was buried in the ash of the plain. Its body reached upward, canted slightly from the vertical, as if it were ready to spring again to the stars.

The rocket launcher had been removed. Now it stood on the plain off to one side of the rocket, small and portable, like some deadly insect. The launcher bothered Crag. He wanted to destroy it—or the single missile that remained—but was deterred by its possible use if the enemy should land another manned ship. In the end he left it where it was.

One of the numerous rills which crisscrossed the floor of the crater cut near the base of the rocket at a distance of about ten yards. It was a shallow rill, about twelve feet wide and ten feet deep, with a bottom of soft ash.

Adam Crag studied the rocket and rill in turn, a plan gradually forming in his mind. The rocket could be toppled, its engines removed and an airlock installed in the tail section, as had been done with the Aztec. It could be lowered into the rill and its body, all except the airlock, covered with ash. Materials salvaged from the drones could be used to construct extensions running along the floor of the rill and these, in turn, covered with ash. This, then, would be the first moonlock, a place where man could live, safe from the constant danger of destruction by chance meteorites.

He looked thoughtfully at the sun. It was an unbearable circle of white light hanging in the purple-black sky just above the horizon. Giant black shadows crept out from the towering walls of the crater. Within another twenty-four hours they would engulf the rocket. During the lunar night —two weeks long—the crater floor would be gripped in the cold of absolute space; the rocket would lie in a stygian night broken only by the brilliance of the stars and the reflected light of an earth which would seem to fill the sky. But they couldn't wait for the advent of a new day. They would have to get started immediately.

Larkwell opposed the idea of working through the long lunar night. He argued that the suits would not offer sufficient protection against the cold, they needed light to work, and that the slow progress they would make wouldn't warrant the risks and discomfort they would have to undergo. Nagel unexpectedly sided with Crag. He cited the waste of oxygen which resulted by having to decompress Bandit every time someone left or entered the ship.

"We need an airlock, and soon," he said.

Crag listened and weighed the arguments. Larkwell was right. The space suits weren't made to withstand prolonged exposure during the bitter hours of the lunar night. But Nagel was right, too.

"I doubt if we could live cooped up in Bandit for two weeks without murdering one another," Prochaska observed quietly. "I vote we go ahead."

"Sure, you sit on your fanny and monitor the radio," Larkwell growled. "I'm the guy who has to carry the load."

Prochaska reddened and started to answer when Crag cut in: "Cut the damned bickering," he snapped. "Max handles the communication because that's his job." He looked sharply at Larkwell. The construction boss grunted but didn't reply.

Night and bitter cold came to Crater Arzachel with a staggering blow. Instantly the plain became a black pit lighted only by the stars and the enormous crescent of the earth—an airless pit in which the temperature plunged until metal became as brittle as glass and the materials of the space suits stiffened until Crag feared they would crack.

Larkwell warned against continuing their work.

"One misstep in lowering Red Dog and it'll shatter like an egg."

Crag realized he was right. Lowering the rocket in the bitter cold and blackness would be a superhuman job. Loss of the rocket would be disastrous. Against this was the necessity of obtaining shelter from the meteor falls. His determination was fortified by the discovery that a stray meteorite had smashed the nose of Drone Charlie. He decided to go on.

The cold seeped through their suits, chilled their bones, touched their arms and legs like a thousand pin pricks and lay like needles in their lungs until every movement was sheer agony. Yet their survival depended upon movement, hence every moment away from Bandit was filled with forced activity. But even the space cabin of Bandit was more like an outsized icebox than a place designed for human habitation. The rocket's insulated walls were ice to the touch, their breaths were frosty streams—sleep was possible only because of utter fatigue. At the end of each work shift the body simply rebelled against the task of retaining consciousness. Thus a few hours of merciful respite against the cold was obtained.

FIRST ON THE MOON

Crag assigned Prochaska the task of monitoring the radio despite his plea to share in the more arduous work. The knowledge that one of his crew was a saboteur lay constantly in his mind. He had risked leaving Prochaska alone before, he could risk it again, but he wasn't willing to risk leaving any of the others alone in Bandit. Yet, Prochaska hadn't found the bomb! Larkwell had worked superhumanly at the task of rebuilding the Aztec—Nagel had saved his life when he could just as easily have let him die. Neither seemed the work of a saboteur. Yet the cold fact remained —there was a saboteur!

Richter, too, preyed on his mind. The self-styled Eastern scientist was noncommittal, speaking only when spoken to. Yet he performed his assigned duties without hesitation. He had, in fact, made himself so useful that he almost seemed one of the crew. That, Crag told himself, was the danger. The tendency was to stop watching Richter, to trust him farther and farther. Was he planning, biding his time, preparing to strike? How? When? He wished he knew.

They toppled Red Dog in the dark of the moon.

Larkwell had run two cables to manually operated winches set about twenty-five yards from the rocket. A second line extended from each winch to the ravine. The ends of these were weighted with rocks. They served to anchor the winches during the lowering of the rocket. Finally a guide line ran from the nose of the rocket to a third winch. Richter and Nagel manned the lowering winches while Larkwell worked with the guide line, with only small hand torches to aid them. It was approximately the same setup used on the Aztec—they were getting good at it. Crag helped until the moment came to lower the rocket, then there was little for him to do. He contented himself with watching the operation, playing his torch over the scene as he felt it was needed.

It was an eery feeling. The rocket was a black monster bathed in the puny yellow rays of their hand torches. The pale light gave the illusion of movement until the rocket, the rocks, and the very floor of the crater seemed to writhe and squirm, playing tricks on the eyes. It was, he knew, a dangerous moment, one ripe for a saboteur to strike—or ripe for Richter.

It was dark. Not an ebony dark but one, rather, with the odd color of milky velvet. The earth was almost full, a gigantic globe whose reflected light washed out the brilliance of the stars and gave a milky sheen to Crater Arzachel. It was a light in which the eye detected form as if it were looking through a murky sea. It detected form but missed detail. Only the gross structures of the plain were visible: the blackness of the rocket reaching upward into the night; fantastic twisted rocks which blotted out segments of the stars; the black blobs of men moving in heavy space suits, dark shadows against the still darker night. The eery almost futile beams of the hand torches seemed worse than useless.

"All set." Larkwell's voice was grim. "Let her come."

Crag fastened his eyes on the nose of Red Dog, a tapered indistinct silhouette.

"Start letting out line at the count of three." There was a pause before Larkwell began the countdown.

"One . . . two . . . three . . ."

The nose moved, swinging slowly across the sky, then began falling.

"Slack off!"

The lines jerked, snapped taut, and the nose hung suspended in space, then began swinging to one side.

"Take up on your line, Richter." The sideward movement stopped, leaving the rocket canted at an angle of about forty-five degrees.

"Okay . . ." The nose moved down again, slower this time. Crag began to breathe easier. Suddenly the nose skidded to the rear, falling, then the rocket was a motionless blob on the plain.

"That did it." Larkwell's voice was ominous, yet tinged with disgust.

"What happened?" Crag found himself shouting into the lip mike.

"The tail slipped. That's what we get for trying to lower it under these conditions," Larkwell snarled. "The damn thing's probably smashed."

Crag didn't answer. He moved slowly toward the rocket, playing his torch over its hull in an attempt to discern its details. He was conscious that the others had come up and were doing the same thing, but even when he stood next to it Red Dog was no more than a black shadow.

"Feel it," Larkwell barked, "that's the only way to tell. The torches are useless." They followed his advice. Crag walked alongside the rocket, moving his hand over the smooth surface. He had reached the tail and started back on the opposite side when Larkwell's voice rang in his ears.

"Smashed!"

"Where?"

"The under side—where she hit the deck. Looks like she came down on a rock."

Crag hurried back around the rocket, nearly stumbling over Larkwell's legs. The construction boss was lying on his stomach.

"Under here." Crag dropped to his knees, then to his stomach and moved alongside Larkwell, playing his beam over the hull. He saw the break immediately, a ragged, gaping hole where the metal had shattered against a small rock outcropping. Too big for a weld? Larkwell answered his unspoken thought.

"You'll play hell getting that welded."

"It might be possible."

"There may be more breaks." They lay there for a moment playing their beams along the visible underside of Red Dog until they were satisfied that, in this section at least, there was no more damage.

"What now?" Larkwell asked, when they had crawled back from under the rocket.

"The plans haven't changed," Crag said stonily. "We repair it . . . fix it up . . . move in. That's all there is to it."

"You can't fix it by just saying so," Larkwell growled. "First it's got to be fixable. It looks like a cooked duck, to me."

"We gotta start back," Nagel said urgently, "oxygen's getting low."

Crag looked at his gauge. Nagel was right. They'd have to get moving. He was about to give the signal to return to Bandit when Richter spoke up.

"It can be repaired." For a moment there was a startled silence.

"How?"

"The inside of the cabin is lined with foam rubber, the same as in Bandit—a self-sealing type designed for protection against meteorite damage."

"So . . . ?" Larkwell asked belligerently.

Richter explained, "It's not porous. If the break were covered with metal and lined with the foam, it would do a pretty good job of sealing the cabin."

"You can't patch a leak that big with rubber and expect it to hold," Larkwell argued. "Hell, the pressure would blow right through."

"Not if you lined the break with metal first," Richter persisted.

The suggestion startled Crag, coming as it did from a man whom he regarded as an enemy. For a moment he wondered if the German's instinct for survival were greater than his patriotism. But the plan sounded plausible.

He asked Larkwell: "What do you think?"

"Could be," he replied noncommittally. He didn't seem pleased that Richter was intruding in a sphere which he considered his own.

Crag gave a last look at the silhouette of the fallen giant on the plain and announced: "We'll try it."

"If it doesn't work, we're in the soup," Larkwell insisted. "Suppose there are more breaks?"

"We'll patch those, too," Crag snapped. He felt an unreasonable surge of anger toward the construction boss. He sucked his lip, vexedly, then turned his torch on his oxygen meter. "We'd better get moving."

CHAPTER 18

COLONEL MICHAEL GOTCH looked at the agent across the narrow expanse of his battered desk, then his eyes fell again to the dockets. Four dockets, four small sheaves of paper, each the capsuled story of a man's life. The names on the dockets were literally burned into his mind: Adam Philip Crag, Martin LeRoy Larkwell, Gordon Wells Nagel, Max Edward Prochaska. Four names, four men, four separate egos who, by the magic of man, had been transported to a bleak haven on another world. Four men whose task was to survive an alien hell until the U.N. officially recognized the United States' claim to sovereignty over the stark lands of the moon.

But one of the men was a saboteur, an agent whose task was to destroy the Western claim to ownership by destroying its occupancy of the moon. That would leave the East free to claim at least equal sovereignty on the basis that it, too, had established occupancy in a lunar base.

The agent broke into his thoughts. "I'd almost stake my professional reputation he's your man." He reached over and tapped one of the dockets significantly.

"The word, the single word, that's what you used to tell me to watch for. Well, the single word is there—the word that spells traitor. I'd gone over his record a dozen times before I stumbled on it." He ceased speaking and watched the Colonel.

"You may be right," Gotch said at last. "That's the kind of slip I'd pounce on myself." He hesitated.

"Go on," the agent said, as if reading his thoughts.

"There's one thing I didn't tell you because I didn't want to prejudice your thinking. The psychiatrists agree with you."

"The psychiatrists?" The agent's brow furrowed in a question.

"They've restudied the records exhaustively, ever since we first knew there was a saboteur in the crew.

"They've weighed their egos, dissected their personalities, analyzed their capabilities, literally taken them apart and put them together again. I got their report just this morning." Gotch looked speculatively at the agent. "Your suspect is also their choice. Only there is no traitor."

"No traitor?" The agent started visibly. "I don't get you."

"No traitor," Gotch echoed. "This is a tougher nut than that. The personality profile of one man shows a distinct break." He looked expectantly at the agent.

"A plant." The agent muttered the words thoughtfully. "A ringer—a spy who has adopted the life role of another. That indicates careful planning, long preparation." He muttered the words aloud, talking to himself.

"He would have had to cover every contingency—friends,

relatives, acquaintances, skills, hobbies—then, at an exact time and place, our man was whisked away and he merely stepped in." He shook his head.

"That's the kind of nut that's really tough to crack."

"Crack it," Gotch said.

The agent got to his feet. "I'll dig him out," he promised savagely.

The drive to rehabilitate Red Dog became a frenzy in Crag's mind. He drove his crew mercilessly, beset by a terrible sense of urgency. Nor did he spare himself. They rigged lines in the dark of the moon and rotated the rocket on its long axis until the break in the hull was accessible.

Crag viewed it with dismay. It was far longer than he had feared—a splintered jagged hole whose raw torn edges were bent into the belly of the ship. They finally solved the problem by using the hatch door of Drone Charlie as a seal, lining it with sheets of foam from Bandit, whose interior temperature immediately plummeted to a point where it was scarcely livable.

Prochaska bore the brunt of this new discomfort. Confined as he was to the cabin and with little opportunity for physical activity, he nearly froze until he took to living in his space suit.

Crag began planning the provisioning of Red Dog even before he knew it could be repaired. During each trip from Bandit he burdened the men with supplies. Between times he managed to remove the spare oxygen cylinders carried in Drone Charlie. There was still a scant supply in Drone Baker, but he decided to leave those until later.

The problems confronting him gnawed at his mind until each small difficulty assumed giant proportions. Each time he managed to fit the work into a proper mental perspective a new problem or disaster cropped up. He grew nervous and irritable. In his frantic haste to complete the work on Red

Dog he found himself begrudging the crew the few hours they took off each day for sleep. *Take it easy*, he finally told himself. *Slow down*, Adam. Yet despite his almost hourly resolves to slow down, he found himself pushing at an ever faster pace. Complete Red Dog . . . complete Red Dog . . . became a refrain in his mind.

Larkwell grew sullen and surly, snapping at Richter at the slightest provocation. Nagel became completely indifferent, and in the process, completely ineffectual. Crag had long realized that the oxygen man had reached his physical limits. Now, he knew, Nagel had passed them. Maybe he was right . . . maybe he wouldn't leave the moon.

When the break in Red Dog was repaired, Crag waited, tense and jittery, while Nagel entered the rocket and pressurized it. It'll work, he told himself. It's got to work. The short period Nagel remained in the rocket seemed to extend into hours before he opened the hatch.

"One or two small leaks," he reported wearily. He looked disconsolately at Crag. "Maybe we can locate them—with a little time."

"Good." Crag nodded, relieved. Another crisis past. He ordered Larkwell to start pulling the engines. If things went right . . .

The work didn't progress nearly as fast as he had hoped. For one thing, the engines weren't designed for removal. They were welded fast against cross beams spread between the hull. Consequently, the metal sides of the ship were punctured numerous times before the job was completed. Each hole required another weld, another patch, and increased the danger of later disaster.

Crag grew steadily moodier. Larkwell seemed to take a vicious satisfaction out of each successive disaster. He had adopted an I-told-you-so attitude that grated Crag's nerves raw. Surprisingly enough, Richter proved to be a steadying influence, at least to Crag. He worked quietly, efficiently, seeming to anticipate problems and find solutions before even Crag recognized them. Despite the fact that he found himself depending on the German more and more, he was determined never to relax his surveillance over the man. Richter was an enemy—a man to be watched.

Larkwell and Nagel were lackadaisically beginning work on the ship's airlock when Prochaska came on the interphones with an emergency call.

"Gotch calling," he told Crag. "He's hot to get you on the line."

Crag hesitated. "Tell him to go to hell," he said finally. "I'll call him on the regular hour."

"He said you'd say that," Prochaska informed him amiably, "but he wants you now."

Another emergency—another hair-raiser. *Gotch is a damn ulcer-maker*, Crag thought savagely. "Okay, I'm on my way," he said wearily. "Anything to keep him off my back."

"Can I tell him that?"

"Tell him anything you want," Crag snapped. He debated taking the crew with him but finally decided against it. They couldn't afford the time. Reluctantly he put the work party in Larkwell's charge and started back across the bowl of the crater, each step a deliberate weighted effort. So much to do. So little time. He trudged through the night, cursing the fate that had made him Gotch's pawn.

Gotch was crisp and to the point. "Another rocket was launched from east of the Caspian this morning," he told him.

"Jesus, we need a company of Marines."

"Not this time, Adam."

"Oh . . ." Crag muttered the word.

"That's right . . . a warhead," Gotch confirmed.

Crag kicked the information around in his mind for a moment "What do the computers say?"

"Too early to say for sure, but it looks like it's on the right track."

"Unless it's a direct hit it's no go. We got ten thousand foot walls rimming this hell-hole."

The Colonel was silent for a moment. "It's not quite that pat," he said finally.

"Why not?"

"Because of the low gravity. Thousands of tons of rock will be lifted. Some will escape but the majority will fall back like rain. They'll smash down over a tremendously large area, Adam. At least that's what the scientists tell us."

"Okay, in four days we'll be underground," he said with exaggerated cheerfulness, "as safe as bunnies in their burrows."

"Can you make it that fast?"

"We'll have to. That means we'll have to use Prochaska. That'll keep you off the lines except for the regular broadcast hour," he said with satisfaction.

Gotch snorted: "Go to hell."

"Been on the verge of it ever since we left earth."

"One other thing," Gotch said. "Baby's almost ready to try its wings."

The atomic spaceship! Crag suppressed his excitement with difficulty. He held down his voice.

"About time," he said laconically.

"Don't give me that blasé crap," the Colonel said cheerfully. "I know exactly how you feel." He informed him that the enemy was proclaiming to the world they had established a colony on the moon, and had formally requested the United Nations to recognize their sovereignty over the lunar world. "How's that for a stack of hogwash?" he ended.

"Pretty good," Crag agreed. "What are we claiming?"

"The same thing. Only we happen to be telling the truth."

"How will the U.N. know that?"

"We'll cross that bridge when we get to it, Adam. Just keep alive and let us worry about the U.N."

"I'm not going to commit suicide if that's what you're thinking."

"You can—if you don't keep on your toes."

"Meaning . . . ?"

"The saboteur . . ." His voice fell off for a moment. "I've been wanting to talk with you about that, Adam. We have a lead. I can't name the man yet because it's pretty thin evidence. Just keep on your toes."

"I am. I'm a grown boy, remember?"

"More than usual," Gotch persisted. "The enemy is making an all-out drive to destroy Pickering Base. You can be sure the saboteur will do his share. The stage is set, Adam."

"For what?"

"For murder."

"Not this lad."

"Don't be too cocky. Remember the Blue Door episode? You're the key man . . . and that makes you the key target. Without you the rest would be a cinch."

"I'll be careful," Crag promised.

"Doubly careful," Gotch cautioned. "Don't be a sitting duck. I think maybe we'll have a report for you before long," he added enigmatically.

"If the warhead doesn't get us," Crag reminded him. "And thanks for all the good news." He laughed mirthlessly. They exchanged a few more words and cut off. He turned to Prochaska, weighing his gaunt face.

"You get your wish, Max. Climb into your spaceman duds and I'll take you for a stroll. As of now you're a working man."

"Yippee," Prochaska clowned, "I've joined the international ranks of workers."

Crag's answering grin was bleak. "You'll be sorry," he said quietly.

CHAPTER 19

THE EARTH was no longer a round full ball. It was a gibbous mass of milk-white light, humpbacked, a twisted giant in the sky whose reflected radiance swept the lunar night and dimmed even the brightest of the stars. Its beacon swept out through space, falling in Crater Arzachel with a soft creamy sheen, outlining the structures of the plain with its dim glow.

Larkwell and Nagel had finished the airlock. The rocket had been tested and, despite a few minute leaks they had failed to locate, the space cabin was sufficiently airtight to serve their purpose. But the rocket had still to be lowered into the rill. Larkwell favored waiting for the coming sun.

"It's only a few more days," he told Crag.

"We can't wait."

"We smashed this baby once by not waiting."

"We'll have to risk it," Crag said firmly.

"Why? We're not that short of oxygen."

Crag debated. Sooner or later the others would have to be told about the new threat from the skies. That morning Gotch had given him ominous news. The computers indicated it was going to be close. Very close. He looked around. They were watching him, waiting for him to give answer to Larkwell's question.

He said softly: "Okay, I'll tell you why. There's a rocket homing in with the name Arzachel on its nose."

"More visitors?" The plaintive query came from Nagel. Crag shook his head negatively.

"We've got arms," Prochaska broke in confidently. He

grinned. "We'll elect you Commander of the First Arzachel Infantry Company."

"This rocket isn't manned."

"No?"

"It's a warhead," Crag said grimly, "a nuclear warhead. If we're not underground when it hits . . ." He left the sentence dangling and looked around. The masked faces were blank, expressionless. It was a moment of silence, of weighing, before Larkwell spoke.

"Okay," he said, "we drop her into the hole."

He turned back and gazed at Red Dog. Nagel didn't move. He kept his eyes on Crag, seemingly rooted to the spot until Prochaska touched his arm.

"Come on, Gordon," he said kindly. "We've got work to do." Only then did the oxygen man turn away. Crag had the feeling he was in a daze.

They worked four hours beyond the regular shift before Crag gave the signal to stop. The cables had been fastened to Red Dog—the winches set. Now it was poised on the brink of the rill, ready for lowering into the black depths. Crag was impatient to push ahead but he knew the men were too tired. Even the iron-bodied Larkwell was faltering. It would be too risky. Yet he only reluctantly gave the signal to start back toward Bandit.

They trudged across the plain—five black blobs, five shadows plodding through a midnight pit. Crag led the way. The earth overhead gleamed with a yellow-green light. The stars against the purple-black sky were washed to a million glimmering pinpoints. The sky, the crater, the black shadows etched against the blacker night bespoke the alienage of the universe. Arzachel was the forgotten world. More, a world that never was. It was solid matter created of nothingness, floating in nothingness, a minute speck adrift in the terrible emptiness of the cosmos. He shivered. It was an eery feeling.

He reached Bandit and waited for the others to arrive. Prochaska, fresher than the others, was first on the scene. He threw a mock salute to Crag and started up the ladder. Larkwell and Richter arrived moments later. He watched them approach. They seemed stooped—like old men, he thought—but they gave him a short nod before climbing to the space cabin. He was beginning to worry before Nagel finally appeared. The oxygen man was staggering with weariness, barely able to stand erect. Crag stepped aside.

"After you, Gordon."

"Thanks, Skipper."

Crag anxiously watched while Gordon pulled his way up the rope ladder. He paused halfway and rested his head on his arms. After a moment he resumed the climb. Crag waited until he reached the cabin before following. Could Nagel hold out? Could a man die of sheer exhaustion? The worry nibbled at his mind. Maybe he should give him a day's rest—let him monitor the communicator. Or just sleep. As it was his contribution to their work was nil. He did little more than go through the motions.

Crag debated the problem while they pressurized the cabin and removed their suits. What would Gotch do? Gotch would drive him till he died. That's what Gotch would expect him to do. No, he couldn't be soft. Even Nagel's slight contribution might make the difference between success or failure. Life or death. He would have to ride it out. Crag set his lips grimly. He had felt kinder toward the oxygen man since that brief period when Nagel had let him peer into his mind. Now . . . now he felt like his executioner. Just when he was beginning to understand the vistas of Nagel's being. But understanding and sympathizing with Nagel made his task all the more difficult. Impatiently he pushed the problem from his mind. There were other, bigger things he had to consider. Like the warhead.

Larkwell was getting out their rations when Prochaska

FIRST ON THE MOON

slumped wordlessly to the floor. Crag leaped to his side. The Chief's face was white, drawn, twisted in a curious way. Crag felt bewildered. Odd but his brain refused to function. He was struggling to make himself think when he saw Nagel leap for his pressure suit. Understanding came. He shouted to the others and grabbed for his own garments. He fought a wave of dizziness while he struggled to get them on. His fingers were heavy, awkward. He fumbled with the face plate for long precious seconds before he managed to pull it shut and snap on the oxygen.

Nagel had finished and was trying to dress Prochaska. Crag sprang to help him. Together they managed to get him into his suit and turn on his oxygen. Only then did he speak.

"How did we lose oxygen, Gordon?"

"I don't know." He sounded frightened. "A slow leak." He got out his test equipment and fumbled with it. The others watched, waiting nervously until he finally spoke.

"A very slow leak. Must have been a meteorite strike."

"Can you locate it?"

Nagel shrugged in his suit. "It'll take time—and cost some oxygen."

Crag looked at him and decided he was past the point of work. Past, even, the point of caring.

"We'll take care of it," he said gently. "Get a little rest, Gordon."

"Thanks, Skipper." Nagel slumped down in one of the seats and buried his head in his arms. Before long Prochaska began to stir. He opened his eyes and looked blankly at Crag for a long moment before comprehension came to his face.

"Oxygen?"

"Probably a meteorite strike. But it's okay . . . now."

Prochaska struggled to his feet. "Well, I needed the rest," he joked feebly.

The leak put an end to all thoughts of rations. They would have to remain in their suits until it was found and repaired. At Crag's suggestion Nagel and Larkwell went to sleep. More properly, they simply collapsed in their suits. Richter, however, insisted on helping search for the break in the hull. Crag didn't protest; he was, in fact, thankful.

It was Prochaska who found it—a small rupture hardly larger than a pea in one corner of the cabin.

"Meteorite," he affirmed, examining the hole. "We're lucky it hasn't happened before."

They patched the break and repressurized the cabin, then tested it. Pressure remained constant. Crag gave a sigh of relief and started to shuck his suit. Richter followed his example but Prochaska hesitated, standing uncertainly.

"Makes you leery," he said.

"The chances of another strike are fairly low," Crag encouraged. "I feel the same way but we can't live in these duds." He finished peeling off his garments and Prochaska followed suit.

Despite his fatigue sleep didn't come easy to Crag. He tossed restlessly, trying to push the problems out of his mind. Just before he finally fell asleep thought of the saboteur popped into his mind. I'll be a sitting duck, he told himself. He was trying to pull himself back to wakefulness when his body rebelled.

He slept.

They prepared to lower Red Dog into the rill. Earth was humpbacked in the sky, almost a crescent, with a bright cone of zodiacal light in the east. The light was a herald of the coming sun, a sun whose rays would not reach the depths of Crater Arzachel for another forty-eight hours.

In the black pit of the crater the yellow torches of the work crew played over the body of the rocket, making it appear like some gargantuan monster pulled from the depths of the sea. It was poised on the brink of the rill with cables encircling its body, running to winches anchored nearby. The cables would be let out, slowly, allowing the rocket to descend into the depths of the crevice. Larkwell on the opposite side of the rill manned a power winch rigged to pull the rocket over the lip of the crevice.

"Ready on winch one?" His voice was a brittle bark, edgy with strain. Nagel spoke up.

"Ready on winch one."

"Ready on winch two?"

"Ready on winch two," Prochaska answered.

"Here we go." The line from Red Dog to Larkwell's winch tautened, jerked, then tautened once more. Red Dog seemed to quiver, and began rolling slowly toward the brink of the rill. Crag watched from a nearby spur of rock. He smiled wryly. Lowering rockets on the moon was getting to be an old story. The cables and winches all seemed familiar. Well, this would be the last one they'd have to lower. He hoped. Richter stood beside him, silent. The rocket hung on the lip of the crevice for a moment before starting over.

"Take up slack." The lines to the anchor winches became taut and the rocket hung, half-suspended in space.

"Okay." Larkwell's line tightened again and the rocket jerked clear of the edge, held in space by the anchor winches.

"Lower away—slowly."

Crag moved to the edge of the rill, conscious of Richter at his heels. The man's constant presence jarred him; yet, he was there by his orders. He played his torch over the rocket. It was moving into the rill in a series of jerks. Its tail struck the ashy floor. In another moment it rested at the bottom of the crevice. They would make it. A wave of exultation swept him. The biggest problems could be whipped if you just got aboard and rode them. Well, he'd ridden this one—ridden it through a night of stygian blackness and unbelievable cold. Ridden it to victory despite damnable odds. He felt jubilant.

But they would have to hurry if they were to get all their supplies and gear moved from Bandit before the warhead struck. They still had to cover Red Dog, burying it beneath a thick coat of ash. Would that be enough? It was designed to protect them from the dangers of meteorite dust, but would it withstand the rain of hell to come when the warhead struck? Wearily he pushed the thought from his mind.

When the others had secured their gear, he gave the signal to return to Bandit. They struck out, trudging through the blackness in single file, following a serpentine path between the occasional rills and knolls scattered between the two ships. Crag swung his arms in an effort to keep warm. Tiny needles of pain stabbed at his hands and feet, and the cold in his lungs was an agony. Even in the darkness the path between the rockets had become a familiar thing.

Despite the discomfort and weariness he rather liked the long trek between the rockets. It gave him time to think and plan, a time when nothing was demanded of him except that he follow a reasonably straight course. There was no warhead, no East World menace, no Gotch. There was only the blackness and the solitude of Crater Arzachel. He even liked the blackness of the lunar night, despite its attendant cold. The mantle of darkness hid the crater's ugliness, erasing its menacing profile and softening its features. He turned his eyes skyward as he walked. The earth was huge, many times the size of the full moon as seen from its mother planet, yet it seemed fragile, delicate, a pale ethereal wanderer of the heavens.

Crag did not think of himself as an imaginative man. Yet when he beheld the earth something stirred deep within him. The earth became not a thing of rock and sea water and air, but a living being. He thought of Earth as *she*. At times she was a ghost treading among the stars, a waif lost in the immensity of the universe. And at times she was a wanton woman, walking in solitary splendor, her head high and proud. The stars were her lovers. Crag walked through the night, head up, wondering if ever again he would answer her call.

He had almost reached Bandit when Nagel's voice broke excitedly into his earphones.

"Something's wrong with Prochaska!"

Crag stopped in his tracks, gripped by a sudden fear.

"What?"

"He was somewhere ahead of me. I just caught up to him . . ."

"What's wrong with him?" Crag snapped irritably. Damn, wouldn't the man stop beating around the bush?

"He's collapsed."

"Coming," Crag said. He hurried back through the darkness, cursing himself for having let the party get strung out.

"Too late, Commander." It was Richter's voice. "His suit's deflated. Must have been a meteorite strike."

"Stay there," Crag ordered. "Larkwell . . . ?"

"I'm backtracking too . . ."

They were all there when he arrived, gathered around Prochaska's huddled form. The yellow lights of their torches pinned his body against the ashy plain. Larkwell, on his knees, was running his hands over the electronic chief's body. Crag dropped to his side.

"Here it is!"

Larkwell's fingers had found the hole, a tiny rip just under the shoulder. Crag examined it, conscious that something was wrong. It didn't look like the kind of hole a meteorite would make. It looked, he thought, like a small rip. The kind of a rip a knife point might make. He stared up at Larkwell. The construction boss's eyes met his and he nodded his head affirmatively. Crag got to his feet and faced the German.

"Where were you when this happened?"

"Ahead of him," Richter answered. "We were strung out. I think I was next in line behind you."

Larkwell said softly: "You got here before I did. That would put you behind me."

"I was ahead of you when we started." The German contemplated Larkwell calmly. "I didn't see you pass me."

Crag turned to Nagel. "Where were you, Gordon?"

"At the rear, as usual." His voice was bitter.

"How far was Prochaska ahead of you?"

"I wouldn't know." He looked away into the blackness, then back to Crag. "Would you expect me to?"

Crag debated. Clearly he wasn't getting anywhere with the interrogation. He looked at Nagel. The man seemed on the verge of collapse.

"We'll carry Max back. Lend a hand, Richter." His voice turned cold. "I want to examine that rip in the light."

The German nodded calmly.

"Stay together," Crag barked. "No stringing out. Larkwell, you lead the way."

"Okay." The construction boss started toward Bandit. Nagel fell in at his heels. Crag and Richter, carrying Prochaska's body between them, brought up at the rear.

It took the last of Crag's strength before they managed to get the body into the space cabin.

The men were silent while he conducted his examination. He removed the dead man's space suit, then stripped the clothing from the upper portion of his body, examining the flesh in the area where the suit had been punctured. The skin was unmarked. He studied the rip carefully. It was a clean slit.

"No meteorite," he said, getting to his feet. His voice was cold, dangerously low. Larkwell's face was grim. Nagel wore a dazed, almost uncomprehending expression. Richter looked thoughtful. Crag's face was an icy mask but his thoughts were chaotic. Fear crept into his mind. This was the danger Gotch had warned him of.

Richter? The saboteur? His eyes swung from man to man, coming finally to rest on the German. While he weighed the problem, one part of his mind told him a warhead was scorching down from the skies. Time was running out. He came to a decision. He ordered Larkwell and Richter to strip the pressure gear from Prochaska's body and carry it down to the plain.

"We'll bury him later—after the warhead."

"If we're here," Larkwell observed.

"I have every intention of being here," Crag said evenly.

CHAPTER 20

THE DAY of the warhead arrived.

The earth was a thin crescent in the sky whose light no longer paled the stars. They gleamed, hard and brittle against the purple-black of space, the reds and yellows and brilliant hot blues of suns lying at unimaginable distances in the vast box of the universe. Night still gripped Crater Arzachel with its intolerable cold, but a zodiacal light in the sky whispered of a lunar dawn to come. Measured against the incalculable scale of space distances the rocket had but a relative inch to cross. That inch was almost crossed. The rocket's speed had dropped to a mere crawl before it entered the moon's gravitational field; then it had picked up again, moving ever faster toward its rendezvous with destruction. Now it was storming down into the face of the land.

They buried Red Dog. Larkwell had improvised a crude scraper made of metal strips from the interior of Drone Baker to aid in the task. He attached loops of cable to pull it. Crag, Larkwell and Richter wearily dragged the scraper across the plain, heaping the ash into piles, while Nagel handled the easier job of pushing them over the edge of the rill.

The unevenness of the plain and occasional rock outcroppings made the work exasperatingly slow. Crag fumed but there was little he could do to rectify the situation. It took the better part of eight hours before the rill was filled level with the plain, with only the extreme end of the tail containing the airlock being left accessible.

"Won't do a damn bit of good if anything big comes down," Larkwell observed when they had finished.

"There's not much chance of a major hit," Crag conjectured. "It's the small stuff that worries me."

"Bandit would be just as safe," Larkwell persisted.

"Perhaps." He turned away from the construction boss. Richter was swinging his arms and stamping his feet in an effort to keep warm. Nagel sat dejectedly on a rock, head buried in his arms. Crag felt a momentary pity for him— a pity tinged with resentment. Nagel was the weak link in their armor—a threat to their safety. For all practical purposes two men—he didn't include Richter—were doing the work of three. Yet, he thought, he couldn't exclude the German. The oxygen and supplies he consumed were less than those they had obtained from Bandit and Red Dog. And Richter worked—worked with a calm, relentless purpose—more than made up for Nagel's inability to shoulder his share. Maybe Richter was a blessing in disguise. He smiled grimly at the thought. But we're all shot, he told himself—all damned tired. Someone had to be the first to cave in. So why not Nagel?

He looked skyward. The stars reminded him of glittering chunks of ice in some celestial freezebox. He moved his arms vigorously, conscious of the bitter cold gnawing at his bones—sharp needles stabbing his arms and legs. He was cold, yet his body felt clammy. He became conscious of a dull ache at the nape of his neck. Thought of the warhead stirred him to action.

"We gotta fill this baby," he said, speaking to no one in particular. Oxygen . . . food . . . gear. There's not much time left."

Larkwell snickered. "You can say that again."

Crag said thinly: "We'll make it." He looked sympathetically at Nagel.

"Come on, Gordon. We gotta move."

Crag kept the men close together, in single file, with Larkwell leading. He was followed by Nagel. Crag brought up at the rear. Memory of Prochaska's fate burned in his mind and he kept his attention riveted on the men ahead of him. They trudged through the night, slowly; wearily following the serpentine path toward Bandit. He occasionally flicked on his torch, splaying it over the column, checking the positions of the men ahead of him. They rounded the end of a rill, half-circled the base of a small knoll, winding their way toward Bandit. Overhead Altair formed a great triangle with Deneb and Vega. Antares gleamed red from the heart of Scorpius. Off to one side lay Sagittarius, the Archer. He thought that the giant hollow of Arzachel must be the loneliest spot in all the universe. He felt numbed, drained of all motion.

"Commander."

The single imperative call snapped him to attention.

"Come quick. Something's wrong with Nagell!"

Crag leaped ahead, flashing his torch. He saw Richter's form bent over a recumbent figure while his mind registered the fact that it was the German's voice he had heard. He leaped to his side, keeping his eyes pinned on Richter until he saw the man's hands were empty. He knelt by Nagel—his suit was inflated! Crag breathed easier. He said briefly: "Exhaustion."

Richter nodded. An odd rumble sounded in Crag's earphones, rising and falling. It took him a moment to realize it was Nagel snoring. He rose, in a secret sweat of mingled relief and apprehension, and looked down at the recumbent form, thankful they were near Bandit.

Larkwell grunted, "Gets tougher all the time."

It took the three of them to get Nagel back to the rocket. Crag pressurized the cabin and opened the sleeping man's face plate. He continued to snore, his lips vibrating with each exhalation. While he slept they gulped down food and freshened up. When they were ready to start transferring oxygen to Red Dog, Nagel was still out. Crag hesitated, reluctant to leave him alone. The move could be fatal—if Nagel were the saboteur. But if it were Larkwell, he might find himself pitted against two men. The outlook wasn't encouraging. He cast one more glance at the recumbent figure and made up his mind.

"He'll be out for a long time," Larkwell commented, as if reading his mind.

"Yeah." Crag replaced Nagel's oxygen cylinder with a fresh one, closed his face plate and opened the pressure valve on his suit. He waited until the others were ready and depressurized the cabin. He climbed down the ladder thinking he would have to return before the oxygen in Nagel's cylinder was exhausted.

Each man carried three cylinders. When they reached Red Dog, Larkwell scrambled down into the rill and moved the oxygen cylinders, which Crag and Richter lowered, into the rocket through the new airlock. They increased the load to four cylinders each on the following trip, a decision Crag regretted long before they reached Red Dog. It was a nightmarish, body-breaking trek that left him staggering with sheer fatigue. He marveled at Larkwell and Richter. Both were small men physically. Small but tough, he thought. Tough and durable.

Nagel was awake, waiting for them when they returned for another load. He greeted them with a slightly sheepish look. "Guess I caved in."

"That you did," Crag affirmed. "Not that I can blame you. I'm just about at that point myself."

Nagel spoke listlessly. "Alpine sent a message."

"Oh?" Crag waited expectantly.

"Colonel Gotch. He said the latest figures indicated the rocket would strike south of Alphons at 1350 hours."

South of Alphons? How far south? It would be close, Crag thought. Maybe too close. Maybe by south of Alphons Gotch meant Arzachel. Well, in that case his worries would be over. He looked at the master chrono. Time for two more trips—if they hurried.

They were making their last trip to Bandit.

Larkwell led the way with Crag bringing up the rear. They trudged slowly, tiredly, haunted by the shortness of time, yet they had pushed themselves to their limit. They simply couldn't move faster.

Strange, Crag thought, there's a rocket in the sky—a warhead, a nuclear bomb hurtling down from the vastness of space—slanting in on its target. The target: Adam Crag and crew. If we survive this . . . what next? The question haunted him. How much could they take? Specifically, how much could *he* take? He shook the mood off. He'd take what he had to take.

He thought: *One more load and we'll hole up.* The prospect of ending their toil perked up his spirits. During the time of the bomb they'd sleep—sleep. Sleep and eat and rest and sleep some more.

Halfway to Bandit he suddenly sensed something wrong. Richter's form, ahead, was a black shadow. Beyond him, Nagel was a blob of movement. He flicked his torch on, shooting its beams into the darkness beyond the oxygen man. Larkwell—there was no sign of Larkwell. He quickened his pace, weaving the light back and forth on both sides of their path.

"Larkwell?" His voice was imperative.

No answer.

"Larkwell?" Silence mocked him. Richter stopped short. Nagel turned, coming toward him in the night.

"Where's Larkwell?"

"He was ahead of me." It was Nagel.

Richter shrugged. "Can't see that far ahead."

Crag's thoughts came in a jumbled train. Had Larkwell been hit by a meteorite? No, they would have seen him fall.

"Must have drawn ahead," Richter observed quietly. There was something in his voice that disturbed Crag.

"Why doesn't he answer?" Nagel cut in. "Why? why?"

"Larkwell! Larkwell, answer me!" Silence. A great silence. A suspicion struck his mind. Crag caught his breath, horrified at the thought.

"Let's get moving—fast." He struck out in the direction of Bandit, forcing his tired legs into a trot. His boots struck against the plain, shooting needles of pain up his legs. His body grew sweaty and clammy, hot and cold by turn. A chill foreboding gripped him. He tried to light the way with his torch. The rocks made elusive shadows—shadows that danced, receded, grew and shortened by turn, until he couldn't discriminate between shadow and rock. He stumbled —fell heavily—holding his breath fearfully until he was reassured his suit hadn't ripped. After that he slowed his pace, moving more carefully. His torch was a yellow eye preceding him across the plain.

Bandit rose before him, jutting against the stars, an ominous black shadow. He moved his light, playing it over the plain. Larkwell—where was Larkwell? The yellow beam caressed the rocket, wandering over its base.

Something was wrong—dreadfully wrong. It took him an instant to realize that the rope ladder had vanished. He swung the torch upward. Its yellow beams framed Larkwell's body against the hatch.

"Larkwell." Crag called imperiously.

The figure in the hatch didn't move. Richter came up and stood beside him. Crag cast a helpless glance at him. The German was silent, motionless, his face turned upward toward the space cabin as if he were lost in contemplation. Crag called again, anger in his voice. There was a moment of silence before a voice tinkled in his earphones.

"Larkwell? There's no Larkwell here." The words were spoken slowly, tauntingly.

Crag snapped wrathfully: "This is no time to be joking. Toss that ladder down and make it quick." The silence mocked him for a long moment before Larkwell answered.

"I'm not joking, Mister Crag." He emphasized the word *Mister*. "There is no Larkwell. At least, not here."

A fearful premonition came to Crag. He turned toward Richter. The German hadn't moved. He touched his arm and began edging back until he was well clear of the base of the rocket. Nagel stood off to one side, seeming helpless and forlorn in the drama being enacted. Crag marshaled his thoughts.

"Larkwell?"

"My name is Malin . . . if it interest you, Mister Crag. Igor Malin." The words were spoken in a jeer.

Crag felt the anger well inside him. All the pent-up emotion he had suppressed since leaving earth boiled volcanically until his body shook like a leaf. The scar on his face tingled, burned, and he involuntarily reached to rub it before remembering his helmet. He waited until the first tremors had passed, then spoke, trying to keep his voice calm.

"You're disturbed, Larkwell. You don't know what you're doing."

"No? You think not?"

Crag bit his lip vexedly. He spoke again:

"So, you're our saboteur?"

"Call me that, if you wish."

"And a damned traitor!"

"Not a traitor, Mister Crag. To the contrary, I have been very faithful to my country."

"You're a traitor," Crag stated coldly.

"Come, be reasonable. A traitor is one who betrays his country. You work for your side . . . I work for mine. It's as simple as that." He spoke languidly but Crag knew he was laughing at him. He made an effort to control his his temper.

"You were born in the United States," Crag pursued.

"Wrong again."

"Raised in the Maple Hill Orphanage. I have your personnel record."

"Ah, that *was* your Martin Larkwell." The voice taunted. "But I became Martin Larkwell one sunny day in Buenos Aires. Part of, shall we say, a well planned tactic? No, I am not your Martin Larkwell, Mister Crag. And I'm happy enough to be able to shed his miserable identity."

"What do you expect to gain?" Crag asked. He kept his voice reasonable, hedging for time.

"Come, now, Mister Crag, you know the stakes. The moon goes to the country whose living representative is based here when the U.N. makes its decision—which should be soon. Note that I said *living*."

"Most of the supplies are in Red Dog," Crag pointed out.

"There's enough here for one man." The voice was maddeningly bland in Crag's earphones.

"You won't live through the rockstorm," Crag promised savagely.

"The chances of a direct hit are pretty remote. You said that yourself."

"Maybe . . ."

"That's good enough for me."

"Damn you, Larkwell, you can't do this. Throw that ladder down." It was Nagel. Again the scream came over the earphones: "Throw it down, I say."

"You've made a mistake," Crag cut in calmly. "We can survive. There's enough oxygen in Red Dog."

"I opened each cylinder you handed down," the man in the hatch stated matter-of-factly. "In fact, I opened all of the cylinders in Red Dog. Sorry, Mister Crag, but the oxygen's all gone. Soon you'll follow Prochaska."

"You did that?" Crag's voice was a savage growl.

"This is war, Mister Crag. Prochaska was an enemy." He spoke almost conversationally. Crag had the feeling that everyone was crazy. It was a fantastic mixed-up dream, a nightmare. Soon he'd awaken . . .

"Coward!" Nagel screamed. "Coward—damned coward!"

The figure in the hatch vanished into the rocket. He's armed! Crag's mind seized on the knowledge that two automatic rifles were still in Bandit. He ordered the men back, alarmed. Nagel stood his ground screaming maledictions.

"Come back, Gordon," Crag snapped.

Malin reappeared a few seconds later holding a rifle. Crag snapped his torch off, leaving the plain in darkness.

"Move back," he ordered again.

"I won't. I'm going to get into that rocket," Nagel babbled. He lunged forward and was lost in the darkness before Crag could stop him.

"Nagel, get back here!" That's an order."

"I won't . . . I won't!" His scream was painful in Crag's ears.

A yellow beam flashed down from the hatch and ran over the ground at the base of the rocket. It stopped, pinning Nagel in a circle of light. His face was turned up. He was cursing wildly, violently.

"Nagel!" Crag shouted a warning. Nagel shook his fist toward the hatch still screaming. Flame spurted from the black rectangle and he fell, crumpled on the plain.

"Move further back," Richter said quietly.

Crag stood indecisively.

Richter spoke more imperatively. "He's gone. Move back—while you can."

"Happy dreams, Mister Crag . . . and a long sleep." The hatch closed.

CHAPTER 21

NAGEL WAS DEAD. He lay sprawled in the ash, a pitifully small limp bundle in a deflated suit. He had gotten his wish—he would never see earth again. *Under the wide and starry sky* . . . Now he was asleep with his dream. Asleep in the fantastically bizarre world he had come to love. But the fact still remained: Nagel had been murdered. Murdered in cold blood. Murdered by the killer of little Max Prochaska. And now the killer was in command! Crag looked down at the crumpled body, reliving the scene, feeling it burn in his brain.

Finally he rose, filled with a terrible cold anger.

"There's one thing he forgot . . ."

"What?" Richter asked.

"The cylinders in Drone Baker. We didn't move them."

He looked at his oxygen gauge. Low. Baker lay almost four miles to the east on a trail seldom used. They had never traversed it by night. Baker, in fact, had become the forgotten drone. He probed his mind. There was a spur of intervening rock . . . rills . . . a twisty trail threading between lofty pinnacles . . .

"We'll have to hurry," Richter urged.

"Let's move . . ."

They started toward the east, walking silently, side by side, their former relationship forgotten. Crag accepted the fact that their survival, the success of his mission—Gotch's well-laid plans—could very well depend upon what Richter did. Or didn't do. He had suddenly become an integral part in the complex machine labeled STEP ONE .

They reached the ridge which lay between them and the drone and started upward, climbing slowly, silently, measuring distance against time in which time represented life-sustaining oxygen. The climb over the ridge proved extremely hazardous. Despite their torches they more than once brushed sharp needles of rock and stumbled over low jagged extrusions. They were panting heavily before they reached the crest and started down the opposite side. They reached the plain and Crag checked his oxygen gauge. The reading alarmed him. He didn't say anything to Richter but speeded his pace. The German's breath became a hoarse rumble in the earphones.

"Stop!" There was consternation in Richter's warning cry. Crag simultaneously saw the chasm yawning almost at their feet.

Richter said quietly: "Which way?"

"Damned if I know." Crag flashed his torch into the rill. It was wide and deep, a cleft with almost vertical sides. They would have to go around it. He flashed the light in both directions along the plain. There was no visible end to the fissure.

He studied the stars briefly and said, "East is to our right. We'll have to work along the rill and gamble that it ends soon."

It did. They rounded its end and resumed their way toward the east. Crag had to stop several times to get his bearings. The shadows danced before the torch beams confusing him, causing odd illusions. He fell to navigating by the stars. It occurred to him that Baker, measured against the expanse of the plain, would be but a speck of dust.

Richter's voice broke reflectively into his earphones, "Oxygen's about gone. Looks like this place is going to wind up a graveyard."

Crag said stubbornly: "We'll make it."

"It better be soon . . ."

"We should be about there."

They topped a small rise and dropped back to the plain. The needle of Drone Baker punctuated the sky—blotted out the stars. Oxygen . . . oxygen. The word was sweet music. He broke into a run, reached its base and clawed at the ladder leading to its hold. He got inside panting heavily, conscious of a slightly dizzy feeling, and grabbed the first cylinder he saw. He hooked it into his suit system before looking down toward the plain. Richter was not in sight. Filled with alarm he grabbed another cylinder and hurried down the ladder. His torch picked up Richter's form near the base of the rocket. He hooked the cylinder into his suit system and turned the valve, hoping he was in time, then flashed his torch on the German's face. He seemed to be breathing. Crag called experimentally into the earphone, without answer. He finally snapped off the torch to conserve the battery and waited, his mind a jumble of thoughts.

"Commander . . . ?"

"Good. I was scared for a moment." He flashed the torch

down. Richter's eyes were open; he was smiling faintly.

"Not a bad way to go," he managed to say. "Nice and easy."

"The only place you're going is Red Dog."

"I'll be okay in a minute."

"Sure you will."

Richter struggled to his feet breathing deeply. "I'm okay."

"We'd better get some more oxygen—enough to last through the fireworks," Crag suggested.

They returned to the drone and procured eight cylinders, lowering them with a piece of line supplied for the purpose. They climbed down to the plain, packed the cylinders and started for Red Dog.

"Going to be close but we'll make it," Crag said, thinking of the warhead.

Richter answered confidently: "We'll make it."

Strange, Crag thought, I wind up fighting with the enemy to keep one of my own crew from murdering me. Enemy? No, he could no longer brand Richter an enemy. He felt a pang of regret over the way he'd mistrusted him. Still, there had been no other course. A thought jolted him. He spoke casually, aware he might be stepping on Richter's toes: "There's one thing I don't understand . . ."

"What?"

"Larkwell's an enemy agent . . ." He hesitated.

"And . . . ?"

"Why didn't he attempt to solicit your aid?" Crag finished bluntly.

"You're a spaceman, Commander, not an intelligence agent."

"I don't get the connection."

"An agent trusts no one. And a saboteur is the lone wolf of the agents. Trust me? Ha! He'd just as soon trust your good Colonel Gotch. No, Larkwell wouldn't have trusted me. Never."

Crag was silent. An agent who couldn't trust a soldier of his own country, even when the chips were down? It was a philosophy he couldn't understand. As for Larkwell! He vowed he'd live long enough to see him dead. More, he'd kill him himself. He was planning how he'd accomplish it when they reached the rill where Red Dog was buried. He switched his torch on and ran it along the edge of the chasm until he located the rope ladder leading down to the airlock.

"You lower 'em and I'll pack 'em." Crag ordered. He descended into the rill and began moving the cylinders Richter lowered to him. Finished, he examined the cylinders they had brought earlier. Empty! His lips set in a thin line as he examined the cylinders which the rocket had brought from earth. Empty . . . all empty. Larkwell had done a thorough job.

He gritted his teeth. Before he was through he'd ram the empty cylinders down Larkwell's throat. Yeah, and that wasn't all. He contemplated the step-by-step procedure. Larkwell would die. Die horribly. He looked toward the hatch wondering what was detaining Richter. He waited a moment, then climbed back to the plain. The German was nowhere in sight.

"Richter?" There was no answer. He checked his interphone to make sure it was working and called again. Silence. He swept his torch over the plain. No Richter. The German had vanished . . . disappeared into the black maw of the crater.

"Richter! Richter, answer me . . . !" Silence. Apprehension swept him. He called again, desperately:

"Richter!"

"I'm all right, Commander." Richter's voice was low,

seeming to have come from a distance. "You'd better get back into Red Dog."

"Where are you?" Crag demanded.

"I have a job to do."

"Come back." The German didn't answer. Crag was about to start in pursuit when he realized he didn't have the faintest idea what direction Richter had taken. He hesitated, baffled and fearful by turn.

Periodically he called his name without receiving an answer. He fumed, wondering what the German had in mind. He couldn't get into Bandit and, besides, he was unarmed. He popped back into Red Dog and looked at the chrono. If Gotch's figures were right the warhead would strike in four minutes. He climbed out of the rill.

"Warhead due in less than four minutes," he called into his mike.

"Get back into Red Dog, Commander," Richter insisted.

Crag snapped irritably: "What the hell are you trying to do."

"Commander, many people have crossed the frontier—from East to West. Many others have wanted to."

"I don't get you."

"I had to come all the way to Arzachel to find my frontier, Commander."

"Richter, come back," Crag ordered, his voice level.

"There's nothing you can do. You didn't know it but when I landed here I crossed the frontier, Commander. I went from East to West, on the moon."

"Richter . . . ?"

"Now I am free."

"I don't know what you're talking about, but you'd better get back here—and pronto. You'll get massacred if you're on the plain when the rocket hits." Inwardly he was shaken. "There's not a damn thing you can do about Larkwell."

"Ah, but there is. He forgot two things, Commander. The oxygen in Baker was only the first."

"And the second?"

Richter did not answer.

Crag called again. No answer. He waited, uncertain what to do next.

The ground twisted violently under his feet. The warhead! A series of diminishing quakes rolled the plain in sharp jolts. Missed Arzachel, he thought jubilantly. It missed . . . missed. He twisted his head upward. The sky was black, black, a great black spread that reached to infinity, broken only by the brilliance of the stars. Off to one side Bettelgeuse was a baleful red eye in the shoulder of Orion.

A picture of what was happening flashed through his mind. Somewhere between Alphons and Arzachel thousands of tons of rock were hurtling upward in great ballistic trajectories, parabolic courses which would bring them crashing back onto the lunar surface. Many would escape, would hurtle through space until infinity ended. Some would be caught in the gravisphere of planets, would crash down into strange worlds. But most would smash back on the moon. Rocks ranging in size from grains of dust to giants capable of smashing skyscrapers would fall like rain.

"Richter! Richter!" He repeated the call several times. No answer. He swept his torch futilely over the plain. Richter was a dedicated man. If the coming rain of death held any fears for him he failed to show it. He looked up again, fancying that he saw movement against the stars. Somewhere up there mountains were hurtling through the void. He hurriedly descended into the rill, hesitated, then moved into the rocket. He again hesitated before leaving the airlock open. Richter might return.

After a while he felt the first thud, a jolt that shook the rocket and traveled through his body like a wave. The floor danced under his feet. He held his breath expectantly, suppressing an instant of panic. The rocket vibrated several times but none of the jolts was as severe as the first. He waited, aware of the stillness, a silence so deep it was like a great thunder. The big stuff must all be down. The thought bolstered his courage. The idea of being squashed like a bug was not appealing. He waited, wondering if Richter had survived. He thought of Larkwell and involuntarily clenched his fists. Larkwell, or Igor Malin—if he lived— would be his first order of business. He remembered Nagel and Prochaska and began planning how he would kill the man in Bandit. He waited a while longer. The absolute silence grated his ears. Now, he thought.

He slipped on a fresh oxygen cylinder, and hooked a spare into his belt, then pawed through the supplies until he found fresh batteries for his torch. Finally he got one of the automatic rifles from Red Dog's arsenal. After that he climbed up to the plain. He called Richter's name several times over the phones, with little hope of answer. He looked at the sky, then swept his torch over the moonscape. A feeling of solitude assailed him. For the first time since leaving earth he was totally alone.

The last time he had experienced such a feeling was when he'd pushed an experimental rocket ship almost to the edge of space. He shook off the feeling and debated what to do. Richter undoubtedly was dead. Had Larkwell —or was it Malin?—survived the rock storm? Spurred to action, he turned toward Bandit. Nothing seemed changed, he thought, or almost nothing. Here and there the smooth ash was pitted. Once he came to a jagged rock which lay almost astride his path. He was sure it hadn't been there before.

He moved more cautiously as he drew near Bandit, remembering that the occupant of the rocket was armed. He climbed a familiar knoll, searching the plain ahead with his torch. He stopped, puzzled, flashing to light to check his bearings. Satisfied he was on the right knoll he played the light ahead again while moving down to the plain. He walked slowly forward. Once he dropped to the ground to see if he could discern the bulk of Bandit against the stars. Finally he walked faster, sweeping the torch over the plain in wide arcs. Suddenly he stopped. Gone! Bandit was gone! It couldn't be. It might be demolished, smashed flat, but it couldn't disappear. He wondered if he were having hallucinations. No, he was sane . . . completely sane. He began calling Richter's name. The silence mocked him. Finally he turned back toward Red Dog.

Crag slept. He slept with the airlock closed and the cabin flooded with oxygen. He slept the sleep of the dead, a luxurious sleep without thought or dream. When he awakened, he ate and donned the pressure suit, thinking he would have to get more oxygen from the drone. He opened the hatch and scrambled out. The plain was light. The sun was an intolerable circle hanging at the very edge of the horizon. He blinked his eyes to get them used to the glare.

He studied the plain for a long time, then hefted the rifle and started toward Bandit before he remembered there was no Bandit. No Bandit? When he reached the top of the knoll, he knew he was right. Bandit unaccountably was gone. He searched the area in wide circles. The question grew in his mind. He found several twisted pieces of metal —a jagged piece of engine. Abruptly he found Richter.

He was dead. His suit hung limp, airless against his body. He stared at the object next to Richter. It was a moment before he recognized it as the rocket launcher.

"He forgot two things, Commander . . ."

Now he understood Richter's words. Now he knew the motive that had driven him onto the plain in the face of the rock storm. Richter had used the launcher to destroy

Bandit, to destroy the murderer of Prochaska and Nagel. He marveled that Richter could have carried the heavy weapon. Once, before, he had watched two men struggle under its weight. Richter must have mustered every ounce of his strength.

He looked at the fallen form for a long time. Richter had crossed his frontier. At last he turned and started toward Red Dog. Adam Crag, the Man in the Moon. Now he was really the Man in the Moon. The only Man. Colonel Crag, Commanding Officer, Pickering Field. General Crag of the First Moon expeditionary Force. Adam Crag, Emperor of Luna. He laughed—a mirthless laugh. Damned if he couldn't be anything he wanted to be—on the Moon.

The sun climbed above the rim of Arzachel transforming the vast depressed interior of the crater into a caldron of heat and glare. In the morning of the lunar day the rock structures rising from the plain cast lengthy black shadows over the ashy floor—a mosaic in black and white. Crag kept busy. He stripped the drones of their scant amount of usable supplies—mainly oxygen cylinders from Baker—and set up a new communication post in Red Dog. In the first hours of the new morning Gotch named the saboteur. Crag listened, wearily. Just then he wasn't interested in the fact that an alert intelligence agent had doubted that a man of 5' 5" could have been a star basketball player, as the Superintendent of the Maple Hill Orphanage had said. He expressed his feelings by shutting off the communicator in the middle of the Colonel's explanation.

The sun climbed, slowly, until it hung overhead, ending a morning which had lasted seven earth days in length. At midday the shadows had all but vanished. He finished marking the last of three crosses and stepped back to survey his work. He read the names at the head of the mounds: Max Prochaska, Gordon Nagel, Otto Richter. Each was followed by a date. Out on the plain were other graves, those of the crewmen of Bandit and Red Dog. He had marked each mound with a small pile of stones. Later it struck him that someday there might be peace. Someday, someone might want to look at one of those piles of stone. He returned and added a notation to each.

The sun moved imperceptibly across the sky. It seemed to hover above the horizon for a long while before slipping beyond the rim. Night seemed eternal. Crag worked and slept and waited. He measured his oxygen, rationed his food, and planned. He was tough. He'd survive. If only to read Gotch off, he promised himself savagely.

The sun came up again. In time it set. Rose and set.

Crag waited.

He watched the silvery ship let down. It backed down slowly, gracefully, coming to rest on the ashy plain with scarcely a jar. Somehow he didn't feel jubilant. He waited, gravely, watching the figures that came from the ship. He wasn't surprised that the first one was Colonel Michael Gotch.

Later they gathered in the small crew room of the Astronaut, the name of the first atom-powered spaceship. They waited solemnly—Gotch and Crag, the pilot, and two crewmen—waiting for the thin man to speak. Just now he was sitting at the small pulldown chow table peering at some papers, records of the moon expedition. Finally he looked up.

"It seems to me that your Nation's claim to the Moon is justified," he said. The words were fateful. The thin man's name was Fredrick Gunter. He was also Secretary-General of the United Nations.